BORN TO BE FREE

Robert Lewis Barros M.D

BORN *to* Be Free

A NOVEL

ROBERT L. BARROS, M.D.

CITIOFBOOKS, INC.
3736 Eubank NE Suite A1
Albuquerque, NM 87111-3579
www.citiofbooks.com
Hotline: 1 (877) 389-2759
Fax: 1 (505) 930-7244

Ordering Information:
Quantity sales. Special discounts are available on quantity purchases by corporations, associations, and others. For details, contact the publisher at the address above.

Printed in the United States of America.
ISBN-13:   Paperback   979-8-89391-250-0
                eBook   979-8-89391-252-4
                Hardback   979-8-89391-251-7

Library of Congress Control Number: 2024916690

In memory of my father

Hernan R. Barros

Carlitos was such a handsome boy. At the age of seventeen, he had finished high school and would be going to London with his father. Since Carlitos was little, his father had been telling him he would go to Cambridge University for college.

His grandfather Fredo had come from a town near Milan, the northern part of Italy. Fredo Calderon had started a mining business in Argentina back in the 1800s.

Fredo was the oldest of four children. His family had a small parcel of land that they shared with some relatives, the Froncheti family. They grew grapes and sold them to the winemakers. Fredo's father also had a shoe repair shop that helped the family get by. Across the courtyard from Fredo's shared house lived the Froncheti family. They had five children. The Fronchetis and the Calderons were like one big happy family. Aside from the fact that they were relatives, they were great friends, and they liked each other's company. Decades before, the big house had been divided to accommodate both families; the Fronchetis had been living in the house with the Calderons for as long as Fredo could remember.

Mr. Froncheri's daughter Rebecca was the prettiest girl in town. Fredo looked at Rebecca like a little sister. She was two years younger than Fredo. Rebecca was different than the rest of the kids. She was truly beautiful and had a charming personality. She moved about like a spring flower, gently moved by the evening breeze. She was her father's favorite, and he always gave her everything she wanted.

The big old house had been built when there was money in the family. Though it was old, it was spacious. There was a big courtyard in the center, and the house was built around the courtyard. There was a large kitchen in the back, and in the room adjacent, without a dividing wall, was a long table open to the air, except the roof, that was made out of Spanish tiles. You could see the tiles from below.

The women loved working in this big kitchen together. Several different generations were there, all sharing with the family their problems and their fortunes, and their dreams for the future. In the back, there was a hundred-acre parcel of land. Years ago, vineyards had been planted by previous generations. Both families depended greatly on the money they made from the fruit of the vine. Once a year, there was a big family effort when the grapes were ripe. They would pick the grapes and place them into these big baskets and transported them via mule and cart to the nearby winery.

Every day, all the neighborhood kids fought and played and laughed and danced together. They were all like brothers and sisters.

Fredo was the oldest in the neighborhood. He was almost eighteen years old and was attending the university. He was very smart, and his parents were very proud of him. They thought that he would be the one to bring progress to the family.

It was time for the yearly event. The grapes had ripened, and the two families had put in motion the great family effort that took place once a year. To get the grapes from the vines to the winery. Every member of the family who was older than ten years contributed to the effort, except, of course, Rebecca. Everyone said she was too pretty and too fragile to do this kind of work, so she stayed behind to look after the youngsters of the family.

Fredo's birthday almost always came when the grapes were ready to be picked and transported to the winery. This year, on the last day of the harvest, was Fredo's birthday. He had chosen to help the family with the grapes, all day; but he went home to take a bath prior to the final trip to bring the grapes to the winery. He wanted to be at the town pub early for his birthday celebration.

There was only one large restaurant-bar in town. Every Friday and Saturday nights and Sundays, all the people from the town would gather at the restaurant to listen to music, socialize, and have some wine and a few beers. It was a place to get together with friends and family, a place to relax, where there was often laughter and music and dancing.

Tonight they were celebrating Fredo's eighteen's birthday. Fredo had invited his friends to the local restaurant, for some drinks, food, and celebration, with music and dancing. It was Saturday night, and the place was full of people from the town. Fredo had invited one of his father's friends to come and play the guitar and sing, to help them make his birthday more festive.

While Rebecca was home looking after the little ones, Alex Calderone, the brother of the mafia boss, comes busting into Rebecca's house without knocking on the door.

Alex said to Rebecca, "Go fix your hair, we are going dancing."

Rebecca said, "I am sorry, I can't go. I have to take care of my little brothers and sisters."

Alex said, "Hurry up, they'll be just fine. Nothing is going to happen to them."

"I can't just go and leave them," said Rebecca.

Alex said, "You know you are dying to be with me. Every woman in this fucking town dreams about me every night, so don't make me tell you again."

"I am not going to go," said Rebecca.

Alex grabbed her two-year-old little brother and squeezed his arm, which made him scream from the pain. "Tell your sister to hurry up and fix her hair," said Alex.

Rebecca ran inside and decided the best thing to do was to

get him out of the house before he hurt one of the little ones, or possibly her.

Rebecca and Alex ran out of the house.

* * *

The night was going well for Fredo, until Alex walked into the restaurant with Rebecca. Fredo was surprised to see Rebecca there. Her family would never let her come to the bar without her father, much less with that good-for-nothing Alex. Rebecca's family was very protective of her. She was her father's darling girl, and he never let her go beyond the corner alone. Fredo remembered that she had stayed home to take care of the little ones.

Alex's brother, Mr. Carleone, was perhaps the most powerful mafia boss in Italy. Fredo was surprised to see Rebecca with Alex.

Rebecca and Alex sat at a table across from Fredo. From the beginning. Fredo could see that there was something wrong. Rebecca looked sad and stressed. She looked as though she was going to cry any minute. She kept looking at Fredo like she was asking for help.

Alex was drinking heavily. He was getting lauder and was being verbally abusive toward Rebecca.

Rebecca kept glancing at Fredo with a desperate look on her face. Fredo was looking at her and wondering what was wrong.

Alex started to notice that Rebecca was looking at Fredo, and he was getting jealous and became more abusive and aggressive. He was obviously upset with Rebecca, as she kept looking at Fredo.

Fredo did not know what to do. Then he finally decided to go and talk to Rebecca.

Fredo walked up to Rebecca and said, "Hi, Rebecca, how you

doing?"

Alex said, "Who the fuck is he?"

Rebecca said, "He is my cousin and neighbor."

Alex said to Fredo, "Get the fuck out of here."

Fredo said, "I just want to talk with Rebecca for a minute."

Alex again said, "Get the fuck out of here now, can't you hear?"

Fredo said, "Relax, man. I just want to talk with Rebecca for a minute."

Alex stood up and took a knife he had hidden in his boot and attacked Fredo. Fredo was frightened and fighting for his life.

Fredo was a man of peace. He never liked to fight. Alex, on the other hand, had the reputation of having killed several men. He and his brother terrorized the town, demanding money from the merchants for "protection," but it was really protection from them.

Alex had been drinking heavily, and was obviously drunk now. Fredo had no choice but to fight with him. Eventually, Fredo took the knife away from Alex and plunged it into Alex's upper left abdomen. Alex fell to the floor, and soon the life was gone from him.

Fredo dropped the knife to the floor and gave Rebecca a kiss on her forehead. Then he ran out of the bar. As he was leaving the bar, Fredo could hear someone say, "Fredo, you are a dead man."

Fredo began to run. He wanted to be gone before the police or the mob arrived.

He ran and ran. All night he ran toward the harbor.

The sun was bringing the morning light. Fredo could see the different boats on the harbor. He was looking for an opportunity to escape. He walked along the docks and found a boat that had an open door to the bridge. No one was around. It was very early in the morning. Fredo quietly walks up the bridge, and enters the ship through the open door. He looked for a place to hide, and finally decided to hide behind some cardboard boxes down below.

Fredo could hear some noise outside. A man was asking questions—had they seen a young man, thin and tall, wearing a white shirt that might have some blood on it?

Fredo, who was hidden in a small hole behind some boxes, immediately took off his bloody shirt. He looked through the boxes and found out that they were exporting Italian clothing to Argentina. He took off his shirt and placed it underneath the boxes. He took a new blue workshirt and put it on.

At the family home, several men suddenly entered, headed by Mr. Carleone. "Where is Fredo?" he asked. "If you do not tell me where he is, I will take each one of these children and break their legs, until you tell me where he is."

Mr. Calderon, who was totally unaware of what had taken place, asked, "What do you want with my son Fredo? We have been taking the grapes to the winery. We just got back. Fredo is supposed to be at the bar. He is celebrating his eighteenth birthday today. You can find him there. Can you please tell me what this is about?"

"Don't act as if you don't know. Rebecca is here. She must have told you what happened!"

"No," said Mr. Calderon. "She arrived only seconds before you did. She was trying to tell me something when you walked through the door." Then he asked his daughter, "Rebecca, what were you going to tell me?"

"This better be quick," said Mr. Carleone.

"Well," said Rebecca, sobbing. "My parents left me here to care for the young children while they harvest the grapes.

"I don't want to hear all that bullshit," said Mr. Carleone. "Tell me, what happened with Alex?"

Alex walked into the house without knocking on the door,

he asked me to go to the bar with him. After hurting my little brother, he forced me to go to the bar with him. We sat right across from Fredo. I was terrified and did not know what to do. Alex was drinking heavily and appeared drunk. He was being verbally abusive to me. Fredo could see my anguish. I was looking at him wondering what to do. Alex was getting angry when he saw me looking at Fredo. Fredo finally got up to talk to me. When he saw Fredo coming to talk with me, he became violent and told Fredo, "Get the fuck out of here."

Fredo said, "I just want to talk to Rebecca for a minute."

Alex pulled a knife and tried to stab Fredo. They fought, and as they were fighting, Fredo was finally able to stab Alex, and Alex fell to the floor dead. Fredo had no choice. He had to defend himself. Fredo ran out afterward. He did not say anything to anyone. We have not seen him since.

"Please, Mr. Carleone, leave us in peace," said Mr. Calderon. "We have not done anything wrong for you to hurt us. Please let the children live without fear, and permit our family to be happy once again."

"We did not ask for this to happen," said Rebecca.

"Okay," said Mr. Carleone. "But if I find out that any member of the family has helped him escape, or continues to have contact with him, you will die with him. Do you understand me?"

"Yes, sir, Mr. Carleone," said Mr. Calderon. What we want most is peace."

* * *

Fredo knew he could never come back. He knew he could never ever have any contact with his family again, because it would put them in severe danger. He must get as far away as possible and never look back. He had considered changing his name. The Italian mob had contacts all over the world and were already looking for him. Fredo was afraid they would find him no matter where he went. In the middle of the night, Fredo took a match and burned his shirt.

The next day, the ship set sail for Argentina. Fredo came out from his hiding place two days later. He was weak and hungry and dehydrated. He had not had any water or food for two days, so he had no choice—he had to come out.

He was brought before the captain. Fredo told the captain, "I am Toni Marcini. I have no money, but I need to get to Argentina. My grandmother is ill there, and I want to see her before she dies. I came in and hid behind your boxes. Please help me." Fredo told the captain he was willing to work. The captain agreed to let Fredo work his way to Argentina. Fredo used a different name, so when the mob started asking questions, his name would not come up. Fredo knew that if he contacted his family, he would be putting them in danger.

Fredo eventually found himself in Argentina. He had been paid for his work on board the ship. He wanted to go to Mendoza, the hub of Argentina's wine industry. He also thought this would be a better place to hide from the mob. So he found some wagons that were going to Mendoza and asked if he could come along. He would pay for his food and help in any way needed along the way. They accepted his proposal.

It was a long way to Mendoza, but Fredo finally arrived.

By now he had used up what little money they had paid him when he left the ship. He was desperate for work.

Fredo walked around town looking for work. He saw several mules loaded with some supplies. He wondered where they were going. There was a man standing next to them, so Fredo decided to ask about the mules. Fredo, who spoke no Spanish, tried to make himself understood. He asked the man, "Where are the mules going?"

The man could not understand what Fredo was saying, so the

man went into the room behind him, and out came another man. This was a well-dressed, tall man, with a sure step and a confident look in his eyes. He asked Fredo what he wanted, and Fredo again tried to ask, "Where are the mules going?"

The man responded in perfect Italian: "You are Italian, aren't you?"

Fredo said, "I am so happy to find someone from Italy here in Argentina. I am Fredo Calderon." He extended his hand.

"I am Luigie Falcon," said the man, shaking hands with Fredo.

"I am happy to meet you," said Fredo.

"It is my pleasure," said Luigie. He asked Fredo, "What are you doing here so far from home?"

"I am looking for a job," said Fredo. "I just got in today. We have been traveling for several days from Buenos Aires. Before that, I was on a ship from Italy."

"Well," said Mr. Falcon, "I could use a hand. I need someone I can trust—are you that man?"

Fredo responded, "Yes, sir, I will do whatever you ask. You won't be sorry. I will help you with whatever you need. It will be a great honor to work for you."

Mr. Falcon said, "I am in the mining business. I will need to go to the Ministry of Mining office to get a permit."

"What is on the mules?" asked Fredo.

"That is our food and medicine and tools that we will need to do the mining. Please look after the mules," said Mr. Falcon, "while I go try to get that permit."

* * *

"Look, Fredo," said Mr. Falcon, this is the map they have provided us, with the mining permit. They have given us a concession larger than I expected, but it is farther away. I figured we could go a little farther and not spend our money on mining fees. I put both of our names on the permit," said Mr. Falcon. "That way, we were able to get a larger area. And if something happens to me, you can continue on."

Fredo said, "That is very generous of you, Mr. Falcon. You won't be sorry."

"Tomorrow morning, we take off for those hills. We will be working very close to the border with Chile. The terrain is rugged, but there is where the minerals are."

Fredo was thinking. *This is really a great opportunity for me. The mob will never find me there.*

Mr. Falcon and Fredo worked long hours every day. The mine yielded tin and cooper. They were also able to get some silver and lead, and even some gold. There was also a lot of iron ore.

Argentina was in the middle of an industrial revolution, and these metals that had been of little use in the past were now being used in great quantities. They could not keep up with the demand."

They started making roads to the mines, and through the mines. They invested on heavy equipment. The demand was greater than their ability to deliver the minerals.

Business was great. They had created the Falcon Calderon Mining Company.

Mr. Falcon turned out to be an honorable, decent man; and that was the way Fredo liked it. Aside from being partners, Fredo and Luigie had developed a deep friendship. They were together all the time. Fredo had great admiration for his friend Luigie. He looked at him as a brother, or at times as a father. Mr. Falcon was ten years older than Fredo, and considered Fredo his only family. Mr. Falcon never mentioned his family, or where he was from. Fredo though that like himself, maybe Mr. Falcon was running from something as well. Neither one of them ever talked about their past. It seemed they both understood that it was an untouchable subject.

Several years had passed, and the mining business was making tons of money for both of them. They had become admired and respected in the community; people looked up to them. They both were able to live a life of pleasure, but neither ever lost sight of hard work.

One spring morning, Luigie was walking to the nearby river to wash his clothes.

Normally, Mariela, the housekeeper took care of his laundry, but she was having another baby. She already had six—this new one made seven. *I wonder why I keep her*, Luigie said to himself. Then he told himself, *Luigie, I know why you keep her! She is the best cook, and she makes your shirts beautiful.* So he decided, *I guess I'll keep her. I'll have to do what I did last year when Mariela had her baby. I will find Mariela's sister to see if she can come and help me until Mariela can come back.*

As Luigie lingered along the path toward the river to wash his clothes, he could not help but to notice that it was a marvelous spring morning. There was an occasional cloud that seemed to decorate the blue ski. The birds too had discovered that spring was in the air. He could see them on top of the trees, showing their newly washed brilliant colors and singing their enchanting songs. They seemed to salute one another as they strutted their feathers and their best songs on this brilliant spring morning.

There were areas of the river that came in and out—these were manmade pools, where a small portion of the river water was diverted into several pools and was used for a variety of domestic purposes. This made it easier for people to approach the river and wash their clothing and themselves and whatever else they wanted to wash, without having to take the risk of going near the fast-flowing river. Aside from the natural beauty of the place, the flowers, the plants, the trees, all in bloom, there was also a great deal of movement of people of all ages, walking about, going to and from the river. Some were going swimming, some to fish, and many women, with large round bags that they carried on top of their heads, to do laundry.

Luigie was pleasantly surprised. He really did not know all of this was there. He knew Mariela went every day to the river to wash his clothes, but he had not taken the time to come to the river before—at least not in this portion of the river, especially on such a beautiful spring morning like today. Luigie came to the edge of one of the pools and had just begun unloading his bag of dirty clothing when a lady came to him and said, "No, sir, please no, don't wash your clothing in this pool. We bathe here. You have to go to the last pool there on the end. There is where we wash our clothes. The water goes back into the river quickly."

"Oh, I am sorry," said Luigie. "I didn't know."

Luigie quickly got his clothing together and moved on to the last pool. When he arrived, he noticed a strikingly beautiful young woman washing her clothes alongside many other women who were also washing clothes. She had golden-brown hair, smooth olive skin, and very large blue eyes. She had obviously been made in heaven with much care, he thought. Luigie stopped to stare. In his head, he was saying, *She is too beautiful to be real.* Suddenly, this young lady stood up and said, "Here, let me help you with that."

She said to Luigie, "You should not be here," she said. "You should have a woman wash your clothes every day. Any woman would be proud to do it."

Luigie did not know what to say or how to react. There appeared to be at least twenty years difference in age between them. He never thought this beautiful young woman could have interest in him. She looked at him with those beautiful blue eyes, and he knew she wanted him. He was stung immediately. He looked at her, and she could see the admiration he had for her. His eyes had opened his soul and his heart to her. He felt the arrow go clean trough his heart. And silently, as she looked into his eyes, she felt the connection, and she too opened her heart to him.

She asked if she could wash his clothes.

He said, "Only if you let me watch you and let me pay you.

"No," she responded, "you can watch me, if you wish. I would love your company, but I cannot accept any money." Then she asked, "What is your name?"

"Luigie," he said. "And yours?"

"My name is Rosa," she said. She took his bag of clothes and started to wash them, as Luigie watched with great admiration her every move.

Rosa was expressive and full of life; she had so much to share. Luigie was more the quiet type, so he listened as this vivacious, enthusiastic, and beautiful girl started to tell him her life story. She told Luigie that she was seventeen years old. She lived with her mother, who made her living washing clothes. "I help her when I can," she said.

"What about your father," asked Luigie.

"I don't remember my father," she said. "He abandoned my mother and me when I was three years old. We lived in a nice house, but my mother had to sell it so that we would survive. My mother married my father against her parents' wishes. My grandparents live in Buenos Aires. They are rich, but they will never, ever again talk to my mother or have any contact with her or help her in any way. They told her that my father was no good, that he was a drunk, had no job, that he would only bring her pain and sorrow, but she married him anyway. My grandfather gave my mother her inheritance the day after the wedding. He told her, 'You are now dead to us. We don't want to ever see you or hear from you again." My mother had been promised in marriage to my uncle Henry. He was to marry my mother when she turned eighteen. She married my dad instead, against her father's wishes, and when the money my grandpa had given my mother had been all spent, my father took off, never to be seen again. My poor mom washed clothes all day so I could finish high school. I just finished high school last week, and after the summer is over, my mother will talk with her boss, so that I can start washing clothes on my own."

Luigie's heart ached upon hearing the story of this girl—this girl to whom he had already handed over his heart.

She asked, "How about you, Luigie? I want to know all about you."

My life is not as interesting as yours, but I do have a long story, and my heart tells me we are going to be spending a lot of time together, and little by little, I will tell it to you. First, I want to talk to your mom to see if she accepts my coming to visit you," said Luigie.

"You will like my mom, and she will like you. How can she not like this tall, strong, handsome man?"

"You know," said Luigie, "I might be about the same age as your mom."

"No, you are probably older. My mom is thirty-five years old. How old are you?"

"I am 36," said Luigie.

"The difference in age is very common in our country," said Rosa.

"It is common in Italy too. I just never thought it would happen to me," said Luigie.

"Luigie," said Rosa, "I have dreamt that someday I would meet a man like you, who would come into my life and love me and protect me and make me feel like a woman, for the rest of my life."

Rosa came by the house every day to pick up Luigie's clothes to be washed. Soon Luigie and Rosa were lovers.

Luigie had been losing weight. He was a chain smoker, and Rosa did not like that about him. He had that constant smoker's cough. He promised to stop, but he had not yet stopped.

Luigie was also worried about his health. He bought a brand-new house for Rosa and her mother. He went to the bank and deposited a large amount of money to be given to Rosa in case of his death.

Fredo had noticed the deterioration in Luigie's health, and he too had spoken with Luigie about going to see the doctor.

Luigie told Fredo he needed to take a couple months off. He thought his weight loss was from the stress at work. "I want to be in full force for your upcoming birthday in two and a half months," he told Fredo.

The real truth was that Luigie wanted to spend every minute of his day with his love, Rosita. They were together all the time—he was with her when she cooked and washed the dishes, they walked down to the river together to wash his clothes, hand in hand they walked along.

Fredo had told Luigi all about his plans for his upcoming twenty-sixth birthday party. Fredo had bought the most beautiful house in town and was very proud of it. He thought his upcoming birthday was the perfect time to show it off.

Luigie had been kind of secretive about his love affair with this young woman, Rosa. He himself felt uncomfortable, and perhaps even ashamed, with the difference in age, but it did not bother her at all. She was proud of her man, and she loved him with all her heart, and she showed him every day with her kindness and her loving ways. Luigie was in heaven. He never knew he could love like this. Often they walked down the pathway to the river hand in hand. She, of course, bubbled with happiness and pride. He worried about what people may be saying, and she laughed at him.

Tonight, Rosita had something very especial to tell him. She told him she had Luigie Junior inside of her.

"What!" said Luigie. "You're pregnant?"

"That's what the doctor said."

"Well," said Luigie, "how do you know it is a boy? Maybe it is a beautiful girl like you. If I had to choose, I would want a girl, but I'll take what the good Lord gives us. It is the happiest moment of my life, ever."

Luigie was thinking. *There are only two days before Fredo's birthday. Fredo does not even know that Rosa exists.*

Fredo had been so busy. He had been in charge of the business, while Luigie had been on vacation. On top of that, he had been planning his birthday party.

Luigie decided that he would wait to tell Fredo about Rosa, after the party. He was going to tell Fredo that he was going to marry Rosa. Luigi would tell Fredo he was going to be a father. He could not wait to tell his best friend the news.

However, knowing that Rosa was expecting his child, Luigie went back to the bank and placed nearly all of his holdings to be given to Rosa by his bank in case of his death.

Luigie was a chain smoker. He rolled his own cigarettes. He had been having these terrible coughing spells and had been bringing up some blood in his sputum. He feared something might happen to him. He had bought a house for Rosa, where they would live after they got married. He had given her some money to keep and made provisions at the bank for her. He told her he wanted her to have the money in case something happened to him.

Eight years had passed since Luigie and Fredo began the mining business. They had worked hard to make their business a success.

Fredo was about to turn twenty-six. He decided it was time to celebrate. He had bought a nice house; it overlooked the vineyards of Mendoza. Fredo thought it was time to get to know his neighbors and all the influential people in town. After all, they had one of the largest businesses in town. He told his friend Luigie of his plans to have a fantastic party to celebrate not only his birthday but their great success in their mining business as well.

Fredo went all out for his party. He brought in from Buenos Aires the best Italian chefs he could find. He brought in entertainers and, of course, the finest Italian music. He hired an interior decorator to do the flowers and arrange his house and the gardens. He got the finest French champagne and Italian wine. He bought himself a tuxedo and invited everyone he knew, as well as his neighbors and business associates.

The party was a great success. It was a perfect night. The stars lit up the sky, and the moon had a small orange border. The smell of flowers was everywhere. There was music and laughter and dancing and gossip. The early morning hours had come and gone; still, the garden was full of dancing and laughter.

Suddenly, Luigie, who had been in the garden with Fredo, began to cough.

This was something common for him, as he was a chain smoker. His fingers were all yellow from the cigarettes, which he rolled himself. He bought Cuban tobacco for his cigarettes, which were a cross between cigars and cigarettes.

Luigi's cough kept getting louder and louder. He turned bright red, and the veins in his neck and forehead stood out, looking like they were going to pop. His cough kept getting more forceful and laud. Fredo brought Luigi inside the house, and sent for the doctor. Luigi could not stop coughing. He was turning purple, and could hardly catch his breath.

Luigi had not told Fredo, but for the past couple of months, Luigi had been coughing up small amounts of blood with his sputum.

Luigi was now turning blue. He couldn't breathe, and then suddenly blood started pouring out of Luigi's mouth and nose. Soon there was a pool of blood on the floor, and Luigi drops to the floor. In a couple minutes, the life was gone from Luigi. The doctor arrived only to confirm that Luigi was dead.

This was very traumatic for Fredo. He had lost not only his best friend and partner, but also the only person he completely trusted and considered family.

Fredo went into a deep depression, and had a hard time accepting the death of his beloved friend. He decided to concentrate on his work. The mining company continued to do well. He decided he wanted to improve himself, so he enrolled in some night classes at the nearby college. He decided to take business administration and accounting courses. He noticed that there was a drama class being offered—it met once a week. They presented a play every year. Fredo decided that this would give him some distraction and keep his mind away from the sadness of his best friend's death, so he decided to enroll.

The first week he attended the night classes, he went to his drama class, but the teacher was ill, and what they got was a substitute that was just filling in. The second week, the teacher was still ill, and again, there was a substitute. Fredo was about to drop the class, but then decided to give it one more week. On the following week, the teacher was finally there. She was a pale, fragile young woman who appeared sad, deep down in her soul. She was very beautiful, but she didn't smile. She looked like she might have had a beautiful smile, but there was something that did not permit her to smile.

Fredo decided to go talk to her after class. He walked up to her desk and said, "My name is Fredo Calderon. I am one of your students."

"How do you do, Mr. Calderon," she said. "I am Maria Perez."

"Ms. Perez," said Fredo, "you look so sad. I want to find a way to make you smile. I bet you have a beautiful smile, but you just don't want to use it. You are afraid you will wear it out."

"That is very kind of you, Mr. Calderon," said Maria, "but that is going to be difficult today."

Fredo picked up a book that had fallen on the floor and places it on her desk. "Ms. Perez, have you had dinner?"

"No, I am not hungry."

"Ms. Perez, you are so thin. You need to eat. Please let me have the pleasure of taking you to dinner."

"I am afraid I would not be very good company," said Ms. Perez.

"I am willing to take a chance," said Fredo.

"Mr. Calderon, I think you are wasting your time with me."

"Let me be the judge of that," said Fredo. "You have to eat, you need to eat, and I promise I will bring a smile to your face."

"Mr. Calderon," she said, "you are very persuasive."

"Good," he says. "I know this Italian restaurant just down the street. They have the best spaghetti in town."

Fredo was older than the rest of Ms. Perez's students. She was probably close to the same age as Fredo. She had just started teaching drama two years ago. Her play from last year had received an award. She was very proud of her accomplishments as a young drama teacher. Aside from being a beautiful woman, she was a great actress. Fredo was taken by her right away. He was amazed by her charm and dynamic personality, which became more evident after he had convinced her to have a couple glasses of wine. He had made her smile after all, and he had never seen a more beautiful smile. She seemed to have forgotten all her problems, and her face would light up with a smile, and she had a thousand stories to tell. But then she would get quiet and wanted to cry.

Fredo and Maria became friends and soon started to go out to dinner frequently. As before, Maria would have a couple glasses of wine, and she would forget her problems. Her enthusiasm for life, her charm, and her laughter would fill the night. Then she would get quiet and sad, and would often cry. Fredo wandered why.

Fredo was delighted with Maria. He could not hide the love he had permitted to enter his heart for her. But he knew there was a deep pain in her soul, and he wondered what made her so sad.

Maria seemed to have frequent doctor's appointments, and Fredo noticed that her family was frequently taking her to the doctor's. Finally, Maria confided in Fredo the truth about her medical condition. She had leukemia, in the early stages; and the doctor had told her that there was no cure, and she had a year, or if she was lucky. two left to live.

Fredo's heart was broken to hear that this beautiful woman he had fallen in love with was going to die. He decided to ask Maria to marry him. One night, as they were walking home under the moonlight, Fredo took Maria's hand and said, "You know, Maria, I have fallen in love with you, and I have decided that I want to marry you."

Maria said, "No, I will not marry you."

"Why, don't you love me?"

"You have your whole life ahead of you," said Maria. "You can have anyone you want. You are handsome and smart and successful. I will only be around for a short time, I don't want to ruin your life in that way. You have been so good to me, and I have never had a better friend, but because I care for you so much, I will have to say no."

Fredo said, "I want to be there for you, to help you through your difficult times. I want to be by your side for the rest of your life. I want to have a child with you. I want a little girl just like you. Someone who will be part of you and part of me. Someone who will be with me long after you are gone." He dropped to his knees and said, "Maria, please marry me. We were meant to be together. You are my destiny, and I will not take no for an answer. Please let me take care of you. Let me love you for the rest of your life. Please don't take that away from me. When you love like I love you, nothing else matters. I just want to be with you every day."

Maria finally decided to marry Fredo. They were married right away, and for the first time in her life, Maria let a man not only into her heart, but also into her body.

Maria got pregnant, and soon they had a baby boy. They named him Ernesto. Fredo was delighted with their little son. He and Maria were very happy together. They both loved him dearly, but soon Maria became debilitated and weak and unable to pick up her dear son. She lost weight and was reduced to skin and bones. Fredo tried to take care of her, but soon Maria was gone; and Fredo once again found himself alone, and this time, he had Ernesto to take care of. He decided he would never again let anyone get into his heart. He would give Ernesto all his love and attention.

Ernesto grew up with all the love and adoration from his father. The years went by, and soon Ernesto was a young man. Fredo sent him to Buenos Aires for university. Ernesto prepared himself to take his place next to his father in the family business.

The mining business continued to improve. Ernesto took over the business. His father had lost interest in the business, and in life. He slept all the time. He was drinking wine all day long. He didn't want to eat. Life seemed to be just a torture for him. He couldn't find happiness. At the age of fifty-eight, Fredo was found dead in his bed. He supposedly died from a heart attack, but his friends thought he died of a broken heart.

*   *   *

Young Ernesto was now alone in charge of the family business. He was very sad and lonely. He started going to the neighborhood bar every night. He found comfort in alcohol. It helped him forget his sadness and his problems, and it helped him sleep at night.

Every night Ernesto was at the bar having his drinks. He always sat at the same place, ordered the same drinks, and at midnight, he went home to sleep.

One night, while Ernesto was at the bar, as usual, an old woman came and sat next to him. "You are the son of Mr. Calderon, aren't you?" she asked.

"Yes, I am," said Ernesto. "I am Ernesto Calderon."

"I knew your father," she said. "He was the best friend of Mr. Falcon."

"My father always talked about his best friend, Mr. Luigi Falcon," said Ernesto.

The old woman said, "Did you know that Mr. Falcon had a daughter?"

"No," said Ernesto, "I didn't know he was married."

"He was not married," she said, "but he had a daughter, Christina. She teaches music at the college."

"How do you know so much about Christina?" asked Ernesto.

"I am her grandmother," the old woman said.

"I would like to meet Christina," said Ernesto. "How do I find her?"

The old woman told Ernesto how to get to Christina's house. The next day, Ernesto put on his best suit, combed his hair, put on his cologne, and instead of going to the bar in the evening, he decided to go to Christina's house. He knocked on the door, and an attractive middle-aged woman answered the door. Ernesto said, "I am Ernesto Calderon, the son of Fredo Calderon."

"I know who you are," said the woman. "My name is Rosa."

"I have come to meet Christina," said Ernesto.

"She is home," said Rosa. "Come in."

Ernesto could hear someone playing the piano in the other room. He looked through the crack on the open door and could see Christina playing the piano.

He was immediately taken by her. Her music penetrated his soul and moved his heart.

"Come," said Rosa, "let me introduce you to my daughter, Christina."

They both walked in to the room, and Rosa said, "Christina, I want you to meet the son of your father's best friend. This is Ernesto Calderon."

Christina stood up and extended her hand.

Ernesto kissed the back of her hand and said, "I am delighted to meet you. Your music is so beautiful, but not as beautiful as your smile."

"That is very kind of you," said Christina.

Christina was two years older than Ernesto, but that did not stop them from falling in love; and six months later, they were married.

Ernesto's life changed drastically. Now he had someone to come home to. He had someone he could share his life with. He bought Christina a big, long piano and loved to spend the nights listening to her play.

* * *

A year later, Christina and Ernesto had a baby boy, and they named him Carlitos. He was the love of their life. Carlitos was a bright, friendly, and happy child. Ernesto and Christina had always wanted a big family; unfortunately, when Carlitos was two years old, he developed the mumps. To his misfortune, Ernesto had never had the mumps as a child, and he ended up sharing the mumps with Carlitos. As is frequently the case with adult males who get the mumps, the infection got into Ernesto's testicles and rendered him infertile for the rest of his life. Christina and Ernesto would never again be able to have another child. Carlitos was everything to them.

Ernesto would tell Carlitos that when it was time for the university, Carlitos was going to go to Cambridge University. Ernesto would tell Carlitos that it was the best university in the world and Carlitos needed to study hard and always be the best in his class so he could go to Cambridge.

Ernesto and Christina would help Carlitos with his studies. From a young age, they got him private English lessons, so Carlitos could learn to speak English well. As an only child, he got the full attention from both parents. This permitted him, to learn much faster than other children his age.

Carlitos graduated from high school as the best student in his class. His parents, of course, were very proud of him, and Ernesto began to plan their trip to Europe. Ernesto would accompany Carlitos to London and get him settled at the university.

Carlitos and his father got on a ship bound for London. Once they got there, Ernesto decided to show Carlitos around.

Together they visited the palace, they went to the museums, to the theater, to the opera, to watch a soccer match, to the parks. Finally, it was time to go to Cambridge, where the university made its home.

Carlitos and his father got the grand tour of the university.

Ernesto did not want his son Carlitos living at the dorm in the university. He didn't want Carlitos making close friends with the rich, snobby kids. Carlitos was so innocent, and Ernesto was afraid that they might corrupt Carlitos, so Ernesto got especial permission for Carlitos to live in a nearby pension where other students also lived. Ernesto paid the caretaker of the pension and asked him to please look after his son.

Ernesto hugged Carlitos and reminded him that he must be the best in his class.

Carlitos took his studies very seriously, and soon he was the best in his class. He was taking business administration, but his hobby was aviation. Though no one had been able to fly a plane, it was just a matter of time, they said. "And we will find a way to fly."

At the pension where Carlitos stayed, there was a young lady named Suzi. She worked at the home doing the cleaning, and she helped prepare the food. She was a happy and friendly person. Suzi was always smiling and frequently whistling as she did her chores. She loved to sing and had a kind word for everyone around.

It was not long before Carlitos started to notice Suzi. He looked forward to seeing her around, singing a tune as she cleaned the floors in the halls or washed the dishes and peeled the potatoes in the nearby kitchen. Carlitos opened his windows every day so he could hear her and could see her as she passed down the hall doing her chores.

Every time she saw Carlitos, she would always ask him how things were going, whether he liked his studies. She would ask him about Argentina, and did he miss being home?

Carlitos loved talking to her, and he looked forward to seeing her every day.

The end of the first school year had come, and it was time

for Carlitos to go home for his summer vacation. He was really looking forward to seeing his parents and being home, and sleeping in his own bed.

He boarded the ship bound for Argentina. He was up on deck looking around as the ship was getting ready to leave. He looked down, and he saw Suzi, who had come to say good-bye. He dammed himself for having come up so soon. He wished he was down below saying good-bye to Suzi. This really touched Carlitos. He yelled down, "Suzi, over here." Suzi looked up and could see Carlitos up on the ship. "Good-bye," she yelled. "I am going to miss you."

"I will miss you too," said Carlitos. "I will write to you."

"I'll write back," said Suzi.

The ship slowly began to move away from the shore. Carlitos was waving to Suzi. She blew him a kiss. Carlitos was thrilled.

* * *

Carlitos was finally home. His parents were anxious to see him. He was delighted to be home. His parents had arranged a party for him. They had invited all his friends and old classmates. Carlitos was thrilled to be home. Every day he had interesting activities for him to enjoy for his vacation; only, it was not summer in Argentina—it was winter, and the days were cold. But Carlitos was happy to be home. He had sent his first letter to Suzi as soon as he got home and had received a letter back from her. Every day he looked to see if there was a new letter for him from Suzi. He wrote to her every day.

He had told his parents about his friend Suzi. He told them that she worked at the home where he lived. She helped the owners of the pension with the work that needed to be done. Ernesto and Christina were a little disappointed. They had hoped that young

Carlitos would find a girlfriend more in keeping with their status. Ernesto told Christina not to say anything derogatory about the girl. "You know young people—they usually do exactly the opposite. This is only his first year. I am sure things will change. The best thing is not to be contrary."

The summer vacation came and went. Carlitos once again found himself in Cambridge, staying at the pension where he stayed the year before. He noticed that Suzi was not there. He waited for a couple of days, but she did not show up. He finally decided to ask the caretaker, Mr. Smith, where Suzi was, and how come she was not around. Mr. Smith said that she had left to be with a relative who had come to pick her up.

This did not sit well with Carlitos. Suzi had told him she had no living relatives, and when her father died, Mr. Smith, who was her father's friend, had taken her in and given her a job and a place to stay. Her mother had died during childbirth, when Suzi was born and she was her father's only child.

Carlitos concentrated on his studies even harder. From childhood, he had been taught strict discipline, and that helped him immensely with his studies. Every day he looked out his window hoping to see Suzi, but he never did. He missed her laughter, her enthusiasm, and her encouraging words. He loved to hear her singing down the hall.

The school year was soon over, and Carlitos found himself once again on the ship bound for Argentina. He remembered the last time he had been on the ship, he had seen Suzi. She had come to say good- bye. He wished he could see her down there again, but he knew she was not coming.

Carlitos spent his summer vacation mostly inside his room, reading and dreaming about Suzi. He wondered if he would ever see her again. He remembered her smile and her kindness. He could not get her out of his mind.

Carlitos entered his third year of college. He returned to the pension and asked Mr. Smith if he had seen or heard from Suzi, or if he knew where she was, or where he could write to her. Mr. Smith said he had not heard from her, and he did not know how to find her.

Again, Carlitos was home for his summer vacation. His parents were concerned about him, because he looked so sad all the time. He didn't want to see his friends. He didn't want to go anywhere. He stayed in his room all day.

Carlitos was on his final year of college. He had made many friends along the way. Many of them had been very kind to him, especially since he was so far away from home. His best friend was David Windford. David had invited Carlitos to spend weekends at David's home on several occasions. David felt sad to see Carlitos so unhappy. Carlitos had confided in David about his friendship and admiration for Suzi. He told David about how she had disappeared, and how the caretaker, Mr. Smith, had told Carlitos that she had been taken by a relative. Carlitos told David that Suzi had said to him that she had no living relatives.

The end of the last year of college finally came. Everybody was excited about graduation. Carlitos, who was the best student in his class, was chosen to give the commencement address.

*   *   *

Mrs. Smith, the wife of the caretaker, was having tea with her friend Matilda. She was telling Matilda the story of Suzi and Carlitos. How Mr. Smith had sent Suzi away. Mr. Smith had found a letter from Carlitos that was sent to Suzi while Carlitos was home on vacation in Argentina. Mr. Smith did not want her mixing with the guests at the pension. He had sent her far away to a country farm owned by Mr. Smith's brother. Young Carlitos, she told Matilda, was to leave for Argentina in the next few days, and they would probably never see him again. Mrs. Smith told Matilda what a fine gentlemen Carlitos had been. He was always buying gifts for them. She told Matilda how sad Carlitos had been since Suzi had gone.

Matilda was moved by the story that Mrs. Smith had told her, and she decided she would investigate and find Suzi. She would try to bring her for Carlitos's graduation. She wanted Carlitos to see Suzi before he would go back home to Argentina.

The graduation ceremony had started. Matilda walked in with Suzi, and they sat on the back row. She had found Suzi working at a farm in the country, and had brought her for Carlitos's graduation.

It was now time for Carlitos to speak. He stood up, walked up to the podium, and delivered his address: "It has been a real adventure, these four years, for all of us. We have entered as boys, and now we graduate as men. Men who will make a difference in this world. Hopefully, men who will stand up for honor and justice. Men who will make this world a better place. These halls have left memories in our minds and in our hearts. I am sure we will never forget them. I know we will always remember our university with pride and respect. I hope we always remember the friends we have made along the way.

"Tomorrow, we will be going home. Some of us have a long way to go. We will never forget the teachers, and fellow students and friends that touched our lives. Some of these friends have made their mark deep in our hearts, and have impacted our lives forever, and we will never forget them."

When the ceremony was over, the graduates filed out to be congratulated by friends and family. As Carlitos was walking out, as he looked in the last row and saw Suzi there. He went to her and put his arms around her. Tears are pouring from his eyes, and Suzi was crying on his shoulder. They stepped outside and walked down to the campus fountain. Carlitos asked Suzi where she had been. She told him about how Mr. Smith had found Carlitos's letters in her room and had sent her to the country to work.

Suzi told him she had no way to escape. She had nowhere to go. No relatives to take her in. She thought if she left without money or a place to go, probably someone would take advantage of her, and she might have ended up being hurt. There were men looking just for such an opportunity. She could not take a chance. "Then Mrs. Matilda Raines came to get me, and that was my chance to escape, and here I am," said Suzi.

Carlitos asks Suzi if she wanted to go home with him to Argentina. Suzi agreed to go, and soon they were on the ship bound for Argentina.

For the first time, Suzi and Carlitos began to really know each other. Suzi told Carlitos about how she was made to feed the pigs and to plow the ground. She thought she would never see Carlitos again. She was beginning to lose hope, until Mrs. Matilda Raines came to get her.

Carlitos and Suzi spent the nights up on deck, dreaming together as they looked at the stars. Carlitos told Suzi how he had admired her the first time he saw her singing down the hall. He told her how he had left his windows open every day hoping to see her again.

Carlitos asks Suzi if she would marry him. Suzi told him that she had been in love with him too. She had lost hope of being with him, and now she wanted to be with him always. She told him she dreamt of waking up every day next to him for the rest of her life.

Little by little, Suzi and Carlitos discovered they were made for each other. They looked forward to the day they would be married, never again to be alone.

Carlitos and Suzi arrived in Argentina, and this time, Carlitos's parents could see a smile in his face. They could see he is really happy. Carlitos introduces his fiancé to his parents.

Carlitos told his parents that he had asked Suzi to marry him. Ernesto and Christina had not seen Carlitos so happy in years. They knew that if she made him so happy, it must be right.

Carlitos and Suzi got married, and soon they had a baby boy they named Carlos Junior. They called him Junior. He became the center of their lives. He was a bright happy child. Carlitos and Suzi were delighted with their son.

Junior really loved his grandparents, and Ernesto spent a lot of time with him. Christina and Ernesto learned to love Suzi. They loved her kind and gentle ways.

When Junior was six years of age, there was an epidemic of smallpox in Argentina. Carlitos and Suzi had been vaccinated in London some years back. In Argentina, many had become infected and died from the disease. Unfortunately, Ernesto and Christina became infected and were taken by the virus. This brought great sadness to Carlitos's home. Junior had a difficult time understanding what had happened to his grandparents, whom he loved so dearly.

Carlitos decided to build a new home. They had been living in the home his grandfather had built many years ago. The house was spacious, but old. Carlitos bought a two-acre parcel of land in the best part of town, where he wanted to build his family home.

Carlitos had Italian marble brought in for the floor of his house. He also had chandeliers brought in from Florence. He had stained glass windows made in Vienna. Carlitos had beautiful gardens made around the house, with fountains and pools and lots of flowers. It had taken nearly two years to build his house.

One night Carlitos and Suzi were invited to have dinner at the house of their next-door neighbor. The neighbors had a fabulous, luxurious home. Carlitos and Suzi were pleased with the invitation. They wanted to get to know their neighbors.

When Carlitos and Suzi came into the neighbors' house, they were given the grand tour. They were impressed by the carpets in the different rooms of the house. The carpets had intricate patterns and beautiful colors that seemed to fit right in with the rest of the room.

Carlitos asked, "Where did you guys get such beautiful carpets?" Federico, the next-door neighbor, said, "We bought them in Bombay, India. We had all the carpets specifically made for each room, with the colors and pattern and size we wanted. They were incredibly inexpensive, and they had so much variety. They let us create our own patterns, and we decided from hundreds of colors exactly what we wanted. Elena and I took a vacation there. We had a great time, and while we were there, they made all the carpets for our house. It was the best thing we did. You know, Carlitos, now that you are decorating your new house, you ought to consider taking a little vacation and at the same time bring back some carpets for your new house. All you have to do is measure the area in each room that you want carpeted and decide what colors and what patterns you want, and just have them make you the carpets just the way you want them,"

It seemed like a great idea to Carlitos. He and Suzi had not taken a vacation since they were married. He decided to put all of his business in order to be able to take a couple months' vacation in India.

Carlitos booked the passage for the three of them. They would take a luxury liner to Bombay, India.

All of the family was excited about the upcoming vacation.

Finally, they were on the ship. Carlitos took Suzi up on deck, and together they remembered how years ago they had looked at the stars together.

Junior came up on deck, and Suzi asked, "Well, did you like your ice cream?"

Junior said, "It was delicious, much better than what we get in Mendoza."

Carlitos and Suzi went back to their room. It was bedtime for Junior. They had made arrangements for a babysitter for Junior; this would give them more freedom to enjoy the evening activities.

Carlitos and Suzi had been invited to dine at the captain's table. The captain had invited all of his most interesting, prestigious, prosperous, influential, and entertaining passengers on board to share the table with him.

Carlitos and Suzi made a handsome couple. Wherever they went, people admired them. They were both very friendly, and soon they were the most popular couple aboard ship. It was a great experience for both of them. During the day, they spent their time with Junior, who loved being in the pool and was fascinated by the ocean and the ship. At night, they had dinner with the captain. There, they listened to the latest gossip, which seemed to get more and more interesting with each bottle of wine.

After dinner, Carlitos and Suzi would go dancing. It was their perfect opportunity to be alone and romantic. They loved it and took advantage of it. After dancing, Carlitos would take a bottle of champagne and take Suzi up on deck to look at the stars and to remember when their love was still tender.

Suzi told Carlitos, "I love you so much more now than I did then."

Carlitos told Suzi, "No doubt, you are my other half."

Eventually, they came ashore in Bombay. It was totally different than they expected. It was very crowded. Fortunately, most of the people spoke English. The British had been in India for many years, and continued to have great influence and presence.

After taking their baggage to their hotel, Carlitos and Suzi decided to walk around and check out the town. They saw venders all over the place, and many stores filled with unusual paraphernalia. Suzi and Carlitos decided to go into one of the stores to look at some decorations. Carlitos asked Junior if he wanted to go in with them. Junior said no, he wanted to stay by the door and watch all the activity on the street. Carlitos said, "Okay, but you have to stay by the door."

Junior said, "Okay."

Junior was distracted by a man that was dancing with the snake around his neck. He stepped out to get a good look. He had never seen anything so strange.

As Junior was looking with total amazement, a man suddenly grabbed him by the arm. He put a rug into Junior's mouth, and with the other hand, he quickly took Junior out. In seconds, he had Junior out of sight and into a cart that was hidden and waiting nearby behind the store. The man wrapped Junior in a sheet and then covered the cart. The mule that was moving the cart suddenly started to move, and soon they were out of the area.

Junior could not make a sound with the rug in his mouth. He could not see anything, either, with the sheet wrapped around him. He could hear the sounds of the mule as the animal walked along the street. Occasionally, the man would give a command, and Junior would notice a reaction from the mule, making the mule turn and eventually stop. They had been traveling about a half an hour. The cart came to a stop. The man tied the sheet around Junior's body with a rope and made a hole below Junior's nose. This allowed Junior to breathe better. Then the man was gone.

* * *

At the shop, Carlitos walked to the door and started to call out Junior's name—at first just softly, thinking he would find Junior by the door. But Junior was nowhere around. Carlitos and Suzi began looking for him all around, calling his name. But they could not find him. They started to get worried and started to yell for him. No response. They asked people around if they had seen him. No one seemed to know where he had gone.

Panic set in with Suzi. Carlitos told her that he was sure they would find Junior. Hours passed, and still they couldn't find Junior. They decided to go to the police and ask for help. They also went to the British magistrate to get their cooperation in finding Junior. The authorities combed the streets; still there was no Junior. Carlitos hired a private investigator and tried to use all the resources available. Suzi gave a picture of Junior to the police. The officers questioned everyone in all the neighborhoods. "Have you seen this boy?" No one seemed to know.

Suzi and Carlitos were devastated. They didn't know where to turn. The darkness began to cover the streets of Bombay. The police advised Suzi and Carlitos to return to their hotel. They told the couple it would be safer for them, and that the police would continue to look for the boy.

Suzi and Carlitos stayed up all night. Suzi's face was swollen from crying all night. The police told them they had no clue where Junior could have gone. No one had seen young Junior disappear.

*   *   *

Junior was left in the cart for several hours. Then he heard the voice of the man that had taken him, as well as the voice of another man. They were speaking in a language he did not understand. Junior could tell the light was disappearing from the day. He could not see much light through the sheet anymore. One of the men picked Junior up and put him up on his shoulder. Junior was all bound by a sheet that had been wrapped around him and tied on.

The man with Junior on his shoulder walked for about three or four minutes, and then the two men seemed to go inside some place. Junior was carried for another four or five minutes before they finally put him on the floor. They took away the sheet that he was wrapped with, and Junior could see the Indian man.

The man said, "You are now my slave. You have been sold to me, and you will live here as a slave. You will do what I tell you, and will speak when I tell you, and if you don't, I will personally beat you until you understand."

"But my parents—" Junior began to say, but suddenly the man slapped him in the face.

"I don't think you understand," said the man. "You will only speak when I ask you to speak, and you will do exactly what I tell you to do."

"But, sir, there is a mistake," said Junior.

The man slapped Junior in the face again. "You don't get it, do you. You are my slave, and you will do exactly what I tell you, and only speak when I ask you to, do you understand me?" Junior was silent. The man slapped him in the face again and said, "Do you understand me?"

Junior said yes.

The Indian men finally left. They gave Junior a blanket and told him to sleep next to one of the boys. Junior discovered that the large room went into another, smaller room. He noticed that there were several other children sleeping on the floor, and there seemed to be some older children sleeping there as well. There was another room in the back, with holes on the floor and the smell of urine and feces.

Junior was in total darkness. As his eyes began to adjust to the darkness, he found a place next to one of the boys and lay down.

*   *   *

Carlitos and Suzi couldn't stop crying. Their precious boy was gone. He couldn't be found anywhere. Days went by, and still they didn't have a clue about Junior. Carlitos had posted a large reward for any information that may lead to finding Junior. But no one had come forward. Weeks went by, and still no news about Junior. After several months, the police told Carlitos and Suzi that it was best if they returned home. Finally, Carlitos and Suzi decide to go home without their beloved Junior.

*   *   *

Junior cried all night long. He couldn't sleep. Morning light came peeking in through the high windows in the room. The boys woke up and immediately prepared themselves for work. The Indian men brought them some bread and a drink Junior had never tasted before.

Junior could not eat. The Indian man said to him, "Eat your bread. It's all you are going to get until midday."

Junior did not know that he had been sold to a man who owned a carpet factory. The man needed young hands to unravel the threads that would be used for weaving the carpets. Only the older, more experienced boys were permitted to do the weaving.

The weaving was complicated. It involved patterns and colors, that had to be done in a precise manner to produce a perfect colorful carpet.

The Indian man came over to Junior and said, "You will never again use your given name. From now on, you will be called Mohamed. You will be punished if you ever use any other name, do you understand me?"

"Yes," said Mohamed.

Every day Mohamed got up at the crack of dawn to unravel the threads. As soon as there was daylight, the owner opened the windows, and Mohamed started to work until the light was gone.

The slaves were beaten frequently. The men gave them barely enough food and water to survive on.

Junior's life changed drastically, and he started thinking of ways to survive this terrible ordeal that had come to him. He never had a moment to rest.

* * *

There was no electricity, no water. We were not allowed to leave the large room where we worked. We could never go out. The large room went into another room where we slept, and led to the bathroom. The bathroom was a hole on the floor, and when we used it, we could hear the urine or feces drop down below. We could not take a bath ever. No brushing our teeth, or combing our hair, or even washing our face.

All the light we had at night came from the candles. They let us have some candles occasionally. We guarded the candles with our lives. We lived mostly in the dark at night. During the days, they opened the windows so we could work with natural light. At night they locked the doors and the windows. We were never permitted to go out. We saw only two men who brought us food and water and materials for work. The only other person that we saw was the man who told us what to do and how to do it, what colors to use, and what patterns. I thought he was the owner.

They would always say ugly and nasty things to us every day. They would tell us, "You are not any better than an animal." They hit us all the time, sometimes without reason. There were about a dozen kids, mostly older than me, who were slaves, without any rights or privilege.

I dreamt of being home in Argentina, in my mother's arm. I had no idea why they had let this happen to me. The days went on, I lost my faith of being free, there was no way out.

They had changed my name. The new name they had given me was Mohamed. No one ever called me by any other name, and as the years went by, I began to forget my real name. We spoke English, and I had not spoken Spanish for years. I started to forget all of that life I had before. I lost all hope and was starting to think this would be my life forever.

* * *

Two years had passed, and Suzi had been in a deep depression. She had not been out of her room. The maid took the food to her room. She had lost weight and had lost all hope of ever seeing her darling son, Junior, again. Carlitos tried to move on.

He asked Suzi to please try again to have another child, but Suzi wanted no part of it. Carlitos was destroyed; his boy was lost forever. But he decided he must move on. As hard as he tried, he couldn't get Suzi to start living a normal life. He decided to move into a separate bedroom.

Carlitos had asked Dr. Arias, the psychiatrist, to come and see Suzi every day. Dr. Arias had given Suzi medication to help her sleep and to take away the severe stress and anxiety she suffered. The doctor had little success with Suzi. She would sleep all day, and she refused to talk to anyone, including Dr. Arias. She wanted no part of life.

One morning, Carlitos entered Suzi's bedroom, opened the drapes, and said, "Enough of this. Come on, get up." He looked at Suzi's pale face—it was white as a sheet. The life had gone from her. Suzi had taken an overdose of sleeping pills and had taken her own life.

She left a note that simply said, "Life is no life without my Junior."

"Carlitos was losing hope". He needed a new life. He wanted to leave it all behind and start a new life somewhere else. He could not live in this home anymore with the memories of his beloved Suzi and his lost son, Junior.

* * *

Eight long years had passed. Mohamed was now sixteen years old, or thereabouts. It was hard to keep track of time. The slaves had no connection with the outside world. Often it was hard to know if it was spring or summer; but they knew when the winter came, because they would almost die with cold. The men did not give them enough blankets to stay warm at night while they slept. Often, the boys would work during the day trembling with cold. When they needed to go to the bathroom, they had to be prepared for a beating, because the men said the boys had to go to the bathroom at night, and not during their working time.

From time to time, a new kid would be brought in—almost always a healthy kid who had no idea what he was in for. Most of them had been sold by their own parents, who already had too many kids and needed the money to survive.

Occasionally, they would take out one of the kids who was found stiff in the morning, dead. This frightened all the boys to no end. It made Mohamed more determined to find a way out.

There he was, about sixteen years old. His parents took him out of the third grade from his school in Argentina to bring him to India, only to be sold as a slave.

* * *

Carlitos wanted to sell his house and the family business and move to San Francisco, California, in the United States, where he wanted to start a new life. He was determined to get into the aviation business. Money was no problem. The Calderon family had been making millions of dollars for decades from the mining business. They had invested their money well in foreign markets and banks, mainly in the USA and Europe.

The last four years since Junior disappeared, Carlitos had concentrated in aviation. Now that Suzi had passed away, he wanted to fulfill his dream. He wanted to get a pilot's license.

Carlitos had read with interest, years ago, before Junior was born, how the Wright brothers had gotten the first plane off the ground a few hundred feet on December 17, 1903. On October 5, 1905, the Wright brothers had the first official airplane flight Carlitos had read that on November 1909, the US government had purchased its first official military plane. Carlitos remembered the year—this was the year that Junior was born. He had read all of this international news with much interest. Aviation was his passion and his dream.

The First World War had come and gone. For the first time in history, the air plane played a significant role in military combat. Carlitos followed with interest all of the news that had to do with aviation. Four years had passed since the disappearance of his beloved son, Junior, and the United States was going through a financial depression. Carlitos desperately wanted to leave this house with all of the memories, and start fresh in a new land, where he could forget all of the sadness in his life.

Most of the manufacturing of airplanes was done in the west coast. The US had manufactured 15,000 planes during the First World War effort. The planes were later being used for moving the mail and for other commercial purpose. The first commercial passenger airline company in the United States was the Boeing

Company out of Seattle, Washington, in 1916. Postwar commercial manufacturing of airplanes in the United States was being done by two companies—the Lockheed Company, which operated out of Santa Barbara, California, and Boeing out of Seatle Washington. The war ended in 1918. In 1922, five years after his son, Junior, had disappeared without a trace, Carlitos finally sold the Falcon Calderon Mining Company, as well as his house. He decided to move to San Francisco. He had passed his exams and gotten his international commercial pilot's license. Carlitos loved to fly. It made him forget all his problems. He was a natural pilot; he understood flying. Carlitos knew what made an airplane fly. He understood the dynamics. He knew how much horsepower an engine needed to lift a given weight. He wanted to design his own planes.

Carlitos was also a good businessman; after all, he had a degree in business administration from Cambridge University. He decided to go back to university, so he enrolled at Stanford University in Palo Alto, California. He studied mechanical engineering and aeronautical engineering. Four years later, he decided to start his own airplane factory.

Carlitos bought a twenty-acre parcel of land in Oakland, California. The land was less expensive there than in San Francisco; and labor was more available, and perhaps less expensive as well. He was fortunate to find a parcel of land that had the Oakland Airport as his next-door neighbor. This made getting into the runway at the Oakland airport easier. Carlitos wanted to make the fastest, most secure commercial planes. He also wanted to have an experimental section, to try new ideas for possible military use. Many of the designs came from Carlitos himself.

Unfortunately, as hard as he tried, Carlitos could not forget about his son, Junior, and his wife, Suzi. He often wondered whatever happened that day in India, where he had lost his beloved Junior. His life had been destroyed forever.

Carlitos decided to train to be a military test pilot. He wanted to learn how to fly the latest and fastest plains. He also decided that all the airplane that came out of his factory would be flight-tested by him.

Carlitos soon had the reputation of being the best test pilot in the United States. The military often asked him to test new experimental military plains, and Carlitos was always thrilled to do it. He loved to fly.

"Junior began to study the possibility of escaping. Where would he go? What would he do for money and food? It would have to be when it was warm. He began to fear that he was forgetting what his mother looked like, or his father. He was forgetting about Argentina. He had not spoken Spanish for more than eight years, and he was afraid he had already forgotten it. Fortunately, India was one of the countries where many of the people spoke English, since they were colonized by the British, so at least he could continue to hear English spoken.

* * *

They did not let us speak very much, and they always speak to us in English.

English was the language in our home in Argentina, since my mother was British. My father also spoke perfect English after his years in Cambridge. When my mother arrived from England, she spoke only English, so when I was born, we spoke English at home; but my grandfather Ernesto, never let me speak English in his home.

Often at night, while I was trying to sleep in the midst of my trembling cold, I would say to myself, *My name is Carlos Calderon, Jr. My mother's name is Suzi, and they call my father Carlitos. I cannot forget that.* I would say it to myself over and over again.

Years had passed, and by this time, I was eighteen years old, or thereabouts. I had not seen a woman since I was eight years old, when I was first sold into slavery.

The days were getting longer, and the nights were getting warmer, and I thought this was the time I must escape. The boys in the room slept better when it was warmer and they didn't have to shake in the cold all night long. I had begun to stay up at night, looking for opportunities to escape.

One afternoon, a man came to visit—the owner of the factory. We could hear them laughing and talking loudly. It was a voice I did not recognize.

These two men had been drinking for several hours. The sun had gone down, and it was time for us to go to sleep. The owner came every night and personally locked the windows and the doors. On this particular night, in his drunkenness, he forgot to bring down the latch in one of the windows. I noticed it right away, and I saw my opportunity to escape. I waited until everyone was asleep. Though I did not know it at the time, the owner and his friend were passed out down the hall in a room near the entrance. I slowly opened the window part of the way. I got up on a chair to look out and then opened the window all the way. The windows were up high. As I looked down, I had no idea that we were on the second floor. I had never looked out the window before, and I never knew that we were on the second floor. It was ten years ago that they had brought me here, all rolled up in a sheet. They never permitted us to get even close to the large windows, and we were beaten if we ever tried to get even close.

There were different kinds of threads that we used to make the carpets inside the room where we worked and slept. I had kept a small piece of candle and a match hidden, in case I had an opportunity to escape. I lit the candle, hoping that no one would wake up. immediately began to weave the threads to make a thin rope. After all, I did not weigh very much.

Then I took the woven threads, and I tied one end to the leg of the large table against the wall. This was the table where they kept all the threads and equipment. I stood up on the chair and climbed up to the window, and then I slowly lowered myself onto the floor on the other side.

When I got on the floor, I didn't know which way to go. There was no one there, it seemed. It was dark, and I couldn't hear or see anything. It was a storage room without a roof. I could not see the moon; the light was blocked by a tree. I tripped over something, got up, then I walked in one direction, but still, I could not see anything, and finally touched a wall. It was very dark. My eyes began to adjust to the darkness, and I was able to see a little better. I finally saw a tiny bit of light on the bottom of the door. I found the door and slowly opened it. It led to an open courtyard. In the courtyard, I noticed the moon was full, and I was able to see better. I could see the cart that the owner's friend had come in. They had left the entrance door open so the visitor could leave whenever he decided to. I hid myself next to the wall and then slowly walked toward the cart, and finally, I was outside on the street.

The street was totally deserted, and in absolute silence and dark, but not so dark because of the moonlight. No one was around. I began to run down the street and under the moonlight. I turned the corner to the right and then ran, and turned to the left, and ran, and turned right again, like the letter Z. I didn't have the strength to run very far. I would hide in the shadows while I rested and then ran again. Far away, I could see some lights. I kept running in the direction of the lights, and soon I could see the ocean and the ships docked along the edge. I sat down on a bench near the ocean, and I fell asleep. I was exhausted, and for the first time in about ten years, I began to smell freedom.

As the sun came up, I was able to see my surroundings better. I started walking around. I saw one of the large boats that had what I thought was the British flag. My father always liked to fly the British flag at home, along with the flag from Argentina. After all, he had gone to school in England and my mother was British. I had not seen the British flag in so long I was not a hundred percent sure it was the British flag. As the morning sun began to warm the day, I started walking toward the ship. When I got near, I could see men loading the ship with all kinds of boxes, large bags, tables, chairs, beds, and other furniture. I was frightened to talk to anyone, so I just hung around and watched for a while.

Suddenly, a very well-dressed man, who appeared to have a military uniform on, came down from the ship. When he got down, he walked toward me, and then he said, "Are you looking for a job, lad? We are short with the help, and we can use an extra pair of hands." Then he said, "You don't look like you are from around here. Where are you from, man?"

I did not know what to say, so I stayed quiet.

"Man, you are skin and bones," said the gentleman.

I just looked down.

"Well, do you want a job or not?" he said.

I said, "Yes."

The gentleman said, "Tomorrow, we take off for England."

I said, "Yes, I very much would like the job."

"I tell you what, lad," he said. "The first thing you will need to do is to take a long bath and get all that dirt off you. Later, the first mate will see you to assign you a job. Now, let's get you some clean clothes. After you clean up, you will be fed and will be assigned a bunk, and later, you will be instructed about your duties, what do you think?"

"I think it's great," I said. I had been looking down the whole time. The Indian man never let me look at him in the face, so I had gotten used to looking down. Since I did not see this gentleman's face, I did not know what he looked like, but I was very glad he had found me.

The man in the uniform called out, "Henry!"

Henry said, "Yes, sir. Take this man down, have him get a good bath, give him the proper clothing and some food. Show him where he will sleep and eat. Show him around."

"Yes, sir," said Henry.

Henry came down and asked me, "What is your name, man?"

"Mohamed, sir," I said.

"Well, Mohamed, come with me."

I was so confused about my name. I had been Mohamed for ten long years, and now I did not really know what my name was.

Henry was a kind man. He said, "Hey, Mohamed, where have you been? You are skin and bones, man."

"I know," I responded.

"You are really dirty. Have you ever taken a bath?"

"No, sir."

"You really stink. I will give you some soap and a washcloth and a towel. Take a bath first, then we will get you something to eat. I would feed you first, I can tell you are hungry, but the men on the ship will kill me if I take you to the mess hall stinking like this."

"It's okay, sir," I said. "I will take a bath first."

As we entered the ship and passed by other men, they would say, "Where did you dig him up? My God, he stinks! Get him out of here. He is stinking up the hall!"

We finally made it to the bathroom. I had not had a bath in ten years. I hoped I knew what to do. Henry took me to a room where there were about ten showers (at that time, I did not even know they were showers or how they worked). Henry said, "Take all your clothes off and put them in this bag. I am going to burn them. Just use any one of the showers there."

I was so embarrassed to take off my clothes and have everyone see me. I was skin and bones.

Henry left for a while, and when he came back after about ten minutes, I still had not taken off my clothes.

"Oh man," said Henry. "What is wrong with you, man! Take off your clothes!"

"It's just that I have never taken my clothes off in front of anyone," said Mohamed.

"Well, you are going to have to get used to it, because we all take showers together."

"I don't know how this works," said Mohamed, "please help me."

"Okay, but first, take off all your damn clothes. I will turn on the shower. Then I will take your clothes to the incinerator. I will be back in a minute. Here's the soap, washcloth, and the towel."

And so I took my first shower, with Henry's help. He was very nice. He said to me, "Don't be afraid. I will help you learn your way around."

Henry took me to the mess hall, where he poured me a glass of milk. Then he took a plate and a fork and a knife and gave them to me. "I'll place the milk on the table, and after you get your food, you can come and eat it here."

I was so embarrassed; I had not used a fork or a knife in ten years. I had forgotten that you eat with a fork and a knife. I was used to eating with my fingers. We never had forks, and for sure, no knives.

Henry placed the glass of milk on the table and then came back to me and said, "Come on, man, don't you know how to serve yourself?"

"I am sorry, Henry, but I have been eating with my hands for ten years."

"It's okay, man." Henry took the plate and said, "Here, you like potatoes? How about some beans? Let's get you some salad and some bread and a piece of meat."

"Henry," I said, "is all of that food just for me?"

"Of course, man. That's nothing. I eat twice as much."

* * *

Mohamed sat at the table. He had not had a glass of milk in ten years, and the food tasted so good. He had not sat at a table to eat for ten long years. He could not eat all of the food on his plate. His stomach had shrunk and could not handle that much food. He began to have a sensation of fullness in his stomach, and he thought he was going to throw up. He stopped eating and hoped he would feel better and not throw up. About half an hour later, he began to feel better. He had eaten only a third of his food, and he knew if he had taken another bite, he would throw it all up.

Henry came in and said, "Well, did you eat? Man, you haven't eaten nothing. Don't you want to get some meat on you?"

"It's just that I am not used to eating so much food," said Mohamed.

"I can tell," said Henry. "Come on, I'll show you around. This here is our snack bar. If you get hungry between meals, you can grab a sandwich or a snack, or maybe a drink. Over here is our playroom, where we can play pool or Ping-Pong, or write letters, or listen to the radio, or watch movies."

"I don't think I have ever seen a movie," said Mohamed.

"Are you kidding, man? Haven't you ever seen a movie?" asked Henry.

"No, I have not."

"Well, tonight, we are showing a movie on the big screen. I

am the one who runs the projector. Let's get going," said Henry. "Over here is the engine room. I don't know where you will be assigned. That area over there is the officers' quarters. You never go there, unless you are invited by an officer. Down here are the bunk beds. I will assign you one near me so I can keep an eye on you. And now, you can lie down and sleep. You look very tired."

*   *   *

Mohamed heard Henry's voice. "Hey, Mohamed," he said. "You have slept the hole night and day. You missed the movie. Man, you should have seen the beautiful chicks."

Mohamed asked, "What are the chicks?"

"You don't know what the chicks are? Oh man, where have you been? The chicks are the girls, man."

"I have not seen a girl in ten years," said Mohamed.

"Man, where have you been?"

"I have been a slave for ten years. I was only eight years old when they sold me to slavery. I just escaped last night."

"You mean two nights ago, because you were here all night last night sleeping."

"It is something else to sleep in a bed, with sheets and blankets. I was really tired. I had been awake for more than thirty-six hours. I slept so deep like I have never done before, without fear or discomfort. I had no idea I had slept so long."

"Wow, that is really something," said Henry. "The first officer came by this morning to meet you, but you looked so tired. He told us to let you sleep all you needed. You have been assigned to KP. That will put some meat on you."

"What is KP?" asked Mohamed.

50

"Oh man, you don't know anything. It's what we call kitchen patrol. You will be working in the mess hall, making food for us."

"Really? That's great! What time is it," Mohamed asked.

"It's 9:00 p.m.," said Henry. "In a little while, everyone will be coming to sleep for the night, and you probably will not be able to sleep."

"I will be able to sleep," said Mohamed. "I have not had a good night's sleep for years, until last night. To sleep on a bed with sheets and blankets, and pillows—wow, what luxury. I have been staying awake every night, thinking of ways to escape, and now I am finally free. Can I go up on deck?" he asked.

"Sure," said Henry, "we set sail this morning. You can probably still see some of the lights onshore."

Little by little, Mohamed began to get used to life on the ship. He did his best at work, and soon his boss started liking him. But Henry became his best friend.

At night, they often went up on deck, and Mohamed would tell Henry about his years as a slave. He would tell Henry that he thought he was from Argentina, but he was not really sure.

"I think when you lose hope, your brain gives up. You become unsure of your memories and your past. You start thinking you have been imagining your past, because if it was true that you had such a great life, then why are you here, being a slave? You ask yourself."

Henry asked about Mohamed's family. Mohamed told him he had not seen them in ten years.

"How did you get from Argentina to India?"

"I am not sure," Mohamed said. "I think we came to India on a boat. It was a long time ago. I just remember that my mother was from England and my father from Argentina, where I think I was born. My parents spoke English at home—that is how I know how to speak English even though I am from Argentina.

I am not sure I can speak Spanish anymore." He added, "When you are a slave for ten years, you forget everything. Your mind is just on survival mode. There is no time for memories. They beat you, they starve you, they withhold water from you, because you might need to go to the bathroom when you are supposed to be working. I am surprised I have not forgotten to talk since we were not permitted to speak very much except at night, with the other kids, and only in whispers, because if they heard you speaking, they came in and beat you.

"We were all so tired at night anyway that we fell asleep immediately. We had no desire to talk. From time to time, one of us would be found dead. They would get angry because he died, and they would take him out like an animal, like it was his fault that he died. Then there were times we were sick. We had no medicines and were made to work sick. I thought I would never get out.

"Hey, Henry, look at me. I am like a different person now. I am able to eat normally. I am gaining weight. I don't look so ugly anymore. My skin is better. I had forgotten what color my hair was. I am beginning to have hope in my heart that maybe someday I can live like a normal person.

"I remember when I first got here, how the sun would hurt my skin, and I could not be around the sun for very long because my eyes would get irritated and red, but now all is normal. Hey, Henry, can l ask you a personal question?"

"Of course, man. We are buddies I tell you everything,"

"Have you ever been with a woman—I mean, intimately?"

"Oh man, Mohamed, haven't you ever been with a woman? I have been with dozens of women," said Henry. "That is the beauty of being a sailor. We stop in different ports, and there are always plenty of women."

"But how do you know what to do with a woman?" asked

Mohamed. "I imagine that sometime during your lifetime, someone told you what to do with a woman. Maybe your father or your brother, or even a friend? I have been a slave since I was eight years old, and when you are eight years old, you don't know anything about a woman, except for your mother."

"Oh man, Mohamed, I am not going to tell you what to do with a woman," said Henry. "But I tell you what, you have been watching the movies we show at night, haven't you?"

"It is the only place I have seen a woman," said Mohamed. "But I don't get it. The other day, remember the movie about a family crossing the country on those wagons?"

"Of course I remember," said Henry. "Don't forget I run the projector."

"You see them kissing, then the woman is pregnant, and they start having kids. I don't understand it," said Mohamed.

"See, to have the baby, first they have to have sex," said Henry.

"What is sex?" asked Mohamed.

"Sex is something between a man and a woman that makes the woman get pregnant, and she later has a baby," said Henry. "Look, Mohamed, I have an idea. I will borrow a porno movie from my friend Bill. I will play it for you on the projector, and you can watch a man and a woman having sex."

"I guess I will have to see it to understand it," said Mohamed, "because the only thing different I see between a man and a woman is that she has longer hair and larger breasts and a different voice, which I didn't even know until I watched my first movie with much curiosity."

"Mohamed," asked Henry, "you want to know what is the difference between a man and a woman? Okay, let me put it this way: the man has a dick—that is what you have between your legs and what you piss through. The woman has a pussy—it's totally different. You will see it clearly on the porno movie."

Mohamed would get up early every morning and go up on deck to breathe the fresh ocean air. He loved the feeling of freedom as the morning breeze played with his hair. He loved to see the sun come up in the morning. He was so happy to be outside and free. He would say to himself, *I will find a way to have a good life. I will try and find my mother and my father. I will study, learn to read, and learn all the wonders of life that I have missed. My destiny is to be free, and now I have a chance to dream big dreams and find ways to make them come true.*

* * *

Every day that went by, I was getting used to being free. At first, in the ship, I was afraid to go very far. I thought I should be confined to the space I felt more secure in. When I went up on deck and felt the ocean air, I wondered if I deserved to be free. I thought of all the other slaves that stayed behind. I felt guilty that it was only me that had escaped. I felt hopeless to help them. I wanted the whole world to know how the poor slaves lived. How they were treated like animals, never having the opportunity to see the moonlight, not able to see the birth of a new morning, never able to see the sunshine reflected on the ocean as the sun comes up to spark the new day. And I would say to myself, *What a beautiful day to be free.*

It took me a while to be able to enjoy the sun. I had been without it for so long. I had to be very careful at first not to damage my skin and my eyes.

I remembered that first morning in Bombay, India, when I first saw the light of the sun and I saw full daylight for the first time in ten years. What a glorious morning it was. Unfortunately, I had to look away from the sunlight. The light hurt my eyes, and I had to be very careful. The sunlight seemed to blind me. My eyes were irritated by the light. It took me a long time to really be comfortable on a beautiful bright morning like today, when my heart told me it was great to be free.

I remembered how sensitive my skin was to the sun. How many times I ended up with blisters all over the exposed areas. But now I felt normal. The sun did not bother me. I was truly free.

The crew was all excited, because tomorrow we would dock at Port Elizabeth, over the southernmost tip of Africa. This would be our first stop on our way to Europe.

So many things went through my mind. For the first time, I would be able to set foot somewhere other than India. For the first time, I would be able to see a woman in person.

My friend Henry had shown me the porno movie. I had no idea what a porno movie was. For the first time, I saw a man and a woman having sex. The movie explicitly showed every part of the woman's body, totally nude. I got to see what a pussy looked like, but the truth was I was not ready to be with a woman. I had been so happy just being free. Being able to see the stars at night. To watch a sunset as it splashed its colors against the ocean.

Every day I found new experiences. How great it is to be free. Perhaps as time went by, I may forget what I had lived through, though I doubted it. I knew I would always appreciate every day of my life as a free man. I would rejoice to see the sun come up. I was finally discovering the peace of a good night's sleep—without fear or pain or cold or illness or distress or hopelessness. My nightmares were getting fewer. I remembered those nights without a friend or the soft voice of my mother. The days when they took away my dignity and made me feel as though I was the trash of the earth.

They took it all from me, and I began to think I was nothing, just the garbage of the world, that I was there because no one wanted me.

We arrived in Port Elizabeth. I was anxious to see for the first time what a woman looked like. I wanted to taste freedom. I wanted to see life outside the dark room in which I had lived for so long. My friend Henry asked me if I wanted to be with a woman. I told him I did not think I was ready. He laughed at me. He told me that I was the only man on the ship that was a virgin. I guessed he was right.

I had so much to learn about life, and especially about human behavior and emotions, which I was not permitted to have.

I needed to find out what was expected of me when I encountered a woman. I wondered what I would feel when I was near her. What would it be like to touch her, to talk to her, to go for a walk with her, to look at the stars with her (after all, I loved coming out on deck every night to look at the stars). This reminded me that I was free, and that I could dream of a life of my own. I wondered what it would be like to smell a woman's perfume. (The men on the ship were always talking about a woman's perfume.) After all, I was just a boy of eight years old in my mind, even though in my body, I was eighteen years old.

I had been trying to decide if I would get off the boat at Port Elizabeth. I didn't know how to behave around people, other than what I had learned here aboard the ship. The only friend I could trust was Henry, and he already told me he was really looking forward to being with a woman.

So I thought about being all alone out there. I didn't know if I was ready. I didn't know if I would get off.

I felt secure here on the ship. It had become my world. A world that I appreciated and loved very much. I was afraid of the uncertainty of being lost again and losing my freedom. I was still not ready to be with a woman. I knew Henry wanted to arrange it for me so I could be with a woman for the first time, but I turned him down. I was still discovering myself.

I was not going to lie, since I saw the porno movie, I had been sexually aroused and had started to masturbate. At first I did not know how to do it, but soon, I experimented, and I learned, and now I did it every night, and I was very good at it. I had to be careful, because I didn't want the others to find out. Sometimes the bed shook a little, and I wondered if I would be discovered.

I desired a woman, but I was afraid to be with her, and so I would wait. I had lots of time to discover the truth about a woman. To feel the touch of a woman. To look in her eyes. To discover if she was sincere.

The other night when we saw this romantic movie, I wanted that woman so bad. After the movie, I went into the bathroom and masturbated. I wondered if I would ever have a beautiful woman like that?

More and more, I thought about women, something that I had never given much thought when I was a slave in India. We never saw them. We never talked about them, and after a while, we just forgot about them.

The very face of my mother began to fade away as I concentrated on survival. We knew we would never see our mothers ever again. Many of us asked ourselves, if our mothers had truly loved us, then why would we be here? The tender, loving memories of child-hood, with a loving mom, which always gave me all I needed, especially her love and her care, had faded. Now that I was here, a slave, I asked myself so many times, *Where is Mom*?

Now, I thought about a woman all the time. I was frightened by the idea. I wanted to find a woman that I could feel comfortable with, but I didn't know when, and if it would happen. I had so much to learn and experience. In a way, I was still eight years old.

I have to discipline myself and not permit anything to get in the way of improving myself. I would work hard, with dedication, discipline and study, and perseverance, to learn whatever I needed to know to have a successful life, I thought. *I want to contribute to my world. I don't know yet where I will fit in, because I have not experienced enough of the world to make a decision, but I know I want to make a difference. I feel like I have the obligation to all the other slaves that were left behind, to show them that I can be somebody, and someday, maybe somehow, I can come back, and help them find their freedom too. Now I know for sure. that a man was meant to be free.*

*   *   *

Henry was on deck again tonight with his favorite friend Mohamed. Henry asked him, "Tell me, Mohamed. You told me that Mohamed is not your real name? You told me that it was a name given to you by your master when you became a slave. You told me that he prohibited you from ever again using your real name, or letting anyone else know what your real name was."

"That's right," said Mohamed. "As time passed, I had to stay awake at night repeating my real name so I would not forget it."

"Really?" said Henry. "Why didn't you tell me your real name?"

"I don't know. I have been so afraid to say it at aloud. It is hard for me."

"Come on, Mohamed. You don't believe someone is going to come here and get you after all of this, do you?"

"It's just, that you don't know what it is to be a slave, Henry. You are property. You do not what you want to do but what you are told to do, and you must be prepared to give your life for your master if you must."

"So you do remember your name?" asked Henry.

"Of course I do."

"Well, tell me, what is your name?"

"My mane is Carlos Calderon, Jr."

"You told me your mother is from England."

"Yes, she is. Her name is Suzi. I have said it a million times. I never wanted to forget it."

"Do you remember her last name before she married your father?"

"I think it was Wilcox."

"Now that we are getting close to British shores, it is important that you remember your mother's last name," said Henry.

"You know, in Argentina, I had my father's and my mother's last names. I remember saying to myself, *My name is Carlos Calderon Wilcox.* I can't remember ever knowing any of my mother's relatives. She never spoke about them. Henry, what is going to happen to me when we dock in London?"

"Well," said Henry, "you are half British, and that is good enough for the Brits."

"How am I going to prove it?" asked Mohamed.

"You know your name. You know your parents' name. Though you were born in Argentina, it is a custom of the Brits when they are living away from home to record the birth of their children with the British consulate, or embassy. I bet you are registered."

"I hope so," said Mohamed.

"Mohamed," said Henry, "this is the last time I want to hear you use that name *Mohamed*. You are Carlos Calderon, not Mohamed. I will tell all aboard the ship to start calling you Carlos. You must bury the name *Mohamed* and put the name *Carlos* back in your head and in your heart. You have a new life, and it is with Carlos, not with Mohamed." Henry hugged Carlos.

Carlos said, "I hope I can get used to this."

"Get used to it. It is the name your parents wanted you to have. You look much more like Carlos than Mohamed to me."

It was the last night together for Carlos and Henry. Carlos

had leaned on his friend, and now he would be alone, and he wondered what would happen to him. As they both sat on the deck looking at the stars, for the last time together, far away, they could see the lights of good old England.

Henry told Carlos he would take the train tomorrow, and he soon would be with his parents and brothers and sisters. He had two daughters, he said. He was never married. His daughters lived with his parents. Henry was really looking forward to seeing his family.

Henry told Carlos, "You will receive a good sum of money when you get off the ship. This should last you for a couple months, until you get a job."

Carlos told Henry, "I am worried about what they will do with me when we arrive. I have no documents. I can barely remember my name. It would be terrible if coming from being a slave I would end up in jail."

"You are not a criminal," said Henry. "Just tell them the truth. Of course, they will probably hold you for a couple days while they investigate. After that, they will probably give you some kind of pass you can use until you get back to your native Argentina."

"I have no documents for Argentina either."

"Your birthday must have been recorded somewhere," said Henry. "They will have to come up with a solution. When they see that you are not a criminal, I am sure they will try to help you."

* * *

When we got to port in London, we waited until all the cargo had been unloaded and all of us had been paid. Then we all filed out through the same door.

The British customs agents, of course, asked for passports and documents, and they all showed their documents. Carlos stayed behind, and when they came to him, he told them, "I have no documents."

"Where are you from?" the officer asked.

"I think I am from Argentina," he said.

"Well, what are you doing on a British ship from India?" the officer asked.

"It is a long story. Please help me," said Carlos. "My name is Carlos Calderon, Jr. I am the son of Carlos Calderon and Susan Wilcox. I think I was born in Argentina."

"Come with me," said the officer.

They took me to another office. A middle-aged man came in to the room. He said, "What did you say your name was?"

My first impulse was to say Mohamed. I was wondering if they would punish me. Then I remembered what Henry had told me. I said, "My name is Carlos Calderon, Jr. My father is Carlos Calderon, and my mother was born in England. Her name was Susan Wilcox before she married my father."

"So tell me, Carlos, how did you get on a ship to England from India?" asked the customs agent.

Carlos said, "Somehow I was taken to India and sold as a slave."

"By your parents?" he asked.

"No, I don't think so," said Carlos.

"Don't you know?" asked the officer.

"Well, I have been a slave for ten long years, since I was eight years old. During that period of time, I concentrated on survival. I am surprised I can remember my name and my parents' name. Through all those years as a slave, I would repeat their names a hundred times. I never wanted to forget them. And here I am, hopefully a free man."

"Mr. Calderon, we have an area for undocumented arrivals. It does not mean you are a criminal. Here we will give you a place to stay and food to eat, until we resolve your case. I must let you know, however, that if you have been involved in criminal behavior, you will be put in jail where the criminals belong."

This was a nice place. They treated me well, like a human being, not like an animal. They gave me food and a bed to sleep in, and at night, they showed movies for us.

Two weeks later, a man called my name. He said, "Is Carlos Calderon here?"

I said, "I am Carlos Calderon."

The man said, "Please come with me." We went down a hall, and he said, "Let's get into this elevator."

I had never been in an elevator before. I did not understand it, but suddenly, the door opened, and we were in a different place. The elevator took us to the twenty-second floor. I had no idea why I was being called. I had these terrible thoughts that the man that owned me had come to claim me. I was frightened. *What will happen to me now?* I wondered. I had been through so much from such a young age. I did not know whom to trust. I wished my good friend Henry was here. *What will happen to me now? Is it not my destiny to be free?* I asked myself.

We walked into a room. An older man was sitting behind the desk. He said to me, "Please sit down." Then he said, "Are you Carlos Calderon, Jr?"

I said, "Yes, sir, I am."

"Are you the son of Carlos Calderon and Susan Wilcox?" he asked.

"Yes, sir, I am."

"How old are you?"

"I think I am eighteen years old."

"You think? Don't you know?"

"Well, sir, I was a slave in India. We had no way of knowing when each year passed. I tried counting the winters, and I think I am eighteen years old. We had no way of knowing the dates for sure. I am sorry, but I don't even know what day I was born. I was bought as a slave at the age of eight, and there are many things I do not remember."

"Well, we have communicated with our embassy in Buenos Aires. Your parents registered your birth with the British Embassy on April 28, 1909. We have found documents that confirm that, in fact, you were born to Carlos Calderon and Susan Wilcox in Argentina.

"We will give you a pass so you can get around until your documents come in. It will probably be about two months. You are free to stay here and eat at the cafeteria until your documents arrive. I think you will be granted British citizenship, thanks to your mom."

They moved me to a different place. They gave me a pass. Which it I could come and go without any problems. I chose to stay back; mostly, I was frightened by the city and did not want to go very far, especially alone. I knew sooner or later, I would have to be on my own.

One night, an officer came in. He knocked on the door to my room and asked, "Can I come in?"

I said, "Yes, of course, come on in."

He asked, "Are you Carlos Calderon, Jr.?"

I said I was.

He said, "Are you the son of Carlos Calderon and Susan Wilcox?"

I said yes, I am.

The man said, "Through our embassy in Buenos Aires, we have been informed that your mother passed away eight years ago. I am very sorry," said the man. "We have been unable to find any information about your father.

"Thank you for the information," I said. I could not hold back the tears. I now knew that my dream of seeing my mother was never going to come true.

I was brokenhearted. Deep in my heart, I had hoped to see the mother I once knew but could not remember. I wondered about my father, and if I would ever see him again.

Finally, my documents were ready. I had been granted a British citizenship. I was finally let out on my own.

I was so happy to finally be free. For once, I began to believe it for sure. I was not Mohamed anymore. I was Carlos Calderon, the son of a British citizen. Though I was frightened to finally be alone, I decided I would be strong and brave, and move on.

I asked myself, *Now that I am free, and on English soil, what will I do to survive?* As I walked around the city, everything seemed so complicated, and difficult to understand. It seemed everyone was in a hurry, and was trying to take advantage of me. I felt totally lost and alone, and without anyone I could trust. I decided to look for a place less complicated. I had a hard time being around so many people in the city. I started to walk away from the city. I wanted to find some peace and quiet. So I walked as far away as I could. I did not want to see the city lights, the traffic, and the noise. I felt lost. I finally walked into the countryside. I felt better there. I began to go from farm to farm, asking if they could use an extra hand. I always told them the truth. "I have no training, but I am willing to work hard and learn. Please give me a chance."

I finally got a job. The man that gave me the job seemed very angry all the time. His wife, too, appeared very unhappy. They argued all the time. They screamed at each other; I thought he was going to hit her.

One rainy day, one of the racehorses had run away from the stables. It was the best horse they owned. They looked for him everywhere but could not find him. Finally, my boss sent us off on horseback through the countryside to find him.

I looked all over the place for the horse, and then decided to go a little farther to see if I could find him. This was a horse of great value.

Perhaps I had gone a little farther than we were normally permitted. I thought maybe the horse had gone farther than he was used to.

Suddenly I heard a voice of panic. I looked around and found a man in the ditch, on the ground. He appeared wounded. He said he had been there for two days.

The man had an obvious fracture to his leg, which appeared to be deformed. His forearm was swollen, and he could not move it. He had been unable to get up. For two days he had laid on the ground hoping for someone to find him and give him a hand. He had the smell of urine and feces on him. He wandered what I was doing in this remote area of the countryside. I told him I was looking for a lost horse, that it was most expensive, and that my employer had sent me to look for it. "I heard you crying out, and I came to see."

The man on the ground was dressed in a fancy uniform. He looked very weak. I came alongside of him and asked him what happened. He said he was hit by tree a branch, which knocked him down from his horse. Then he came rolling down into the ditch. "I was distracted for only a second, and the next thing I knew, I am on the ground with a broken leg. I can't move my leg or my arm, and it hurts for me to breathe."

I got my canteen out and offered him some water.

"Thank you so much," the man said. He had dried blood all over his head and face, and his horse was nearby.

I found a small ax hanging from the saddle of the man's horse. I cut some branches from the trees. I made a rack, I found some rope. and I was able to tie the branches together, and then to the horse. I gently got the man onto the rack. He told me where he lived. It was in the opposite direction that I had to go. I gently and patiently dragged the gentleman home.

His family had been desperately looking for him. They immediately put the gentleman inside a long black car and drove him to the hospital. The man and his family were very thankful, and before they left, they asked where they could find me. I told them where I worked.

* * *

Carlos had never seen such a beautiful mansion, with long, well-tended gardens filled with flowers and fountains and beautiful tall trees.

Carlos rode his horse back to the farm.

By the time he got back, it was dark. They had found the lost horse. His employer wondered where he had been. Carlos told him what had happened, and his employer told him, "I pay you to take care of me and my property, not to go wandering off looking for who you can help. You are fired! You can leave in the morning."

Carlos was out of work once again. He had a little bit of money saved up. He started asking all the farms in the area if they needed some help. All day he walked around looking for work, but had no luck.

The man who had been injured was grateful and impressed by what Carlos had done to get him home. Carlos had saved his life, and this gentleman wanted to know who he was. He had asked Carlos where he lived, and Carlos had told him more or less where it was. Carlos did not have good knowledge of the area since he was a newcomer.

The next day, the gentlemen sent his chauffeur to find Carlos and bring him to the hospital.

His chauffeur was able to find the farm where Carlos said he worked, but they told him that he had been fired because he had been gone without permission. "He just left this morning," they said. The chauffeur asked if they had seen which way he went. One of the men pointed him in the direction Carlos had gone.

The chauffeur thanked him and started driving down the road looking for Carlos.

Suddenly, Carlos saw this long, black car approaching. It looked a lot like the car he had seen at the injured man's house. The chauffeur stopped and said, "You are the man that brought Mr. Windford home, aren't you?"

"Yes," said Carlos. He didn't know that was the man's name. "How is he doing?"

"He wants to see you," said the chauffeur.

"He wants to talk to me?" asked Carlos.

"Yes, he would like to talk to you," said the chauffeur.

Carlos was happy to go see him. He wanted to know how the man was doing. Mr. Windford looked so ill, and weak, and all broken up with dried blood over his head and face the last time Carlos had seen him.

I cannot believe this car. I had never been in a car before, let alone this very long fancy car, thought Carlos. The chauffeur took him to Mr. Windford's room at the hospital. He looked so much better now all cleaned up.

Mr. Windford said to him, "I never got your name."

"I am Carlos Calderon," said Carlos.

"I am David Windford," the gentleman said.

Carlos could not believe how different Mr. Windford looked all cleaned up. No blood on his face, clean clothing, and without the smell of urine and feces.

"Your name sounds very familiar," said Mr. Windford. "It is the same name of a classmate of mine when I was a student at Cambridge in my old college days. He was from Argentina. Carlitos was a great friend to me. He was the best student in our class. I remember he took a girl to Argentina with him. Let's see, what was her name? I remember she showed up at the last minute, just before Carlitos left for Argentina. He took her with him. Let's see, what was her name? Oh, I remember—her name was Suzi. I never knew her last name. I just knew that Carlitos was madly in love with her. He talked about her all the time. For a long time, he could not find her, but then she magically appeared just before he was to leave for Argentina."

Mr. Windford then asked, "Tell me, what are you doing in London?"

"Oh, it is a long story," said Carlos.

"Well, I am here with my leg immobilized, unable to go anywhere. I have all the time in the world. Tell me all about it," said Mr. Windford.

"Well," said Carlos, "I have been lost from my parents since I was eight years old. I just found out my mother died shortly after I was lost. I don't know where my father is."

"I am so sorry about your mother. You must be Carlitos's son," said Mr. Windford. "He was about your age when I knew him, and you look just like him."

"I am so happy to know that I looked like my father, and I am lucky to find someone who knew him. Tell me, what was he like?"said Carlos.

Your father was an exceptional man. He was the best in our class, but he was also gentle and kind and loved by all. He was dedicated to his studies like I have never seen anyone. He was a man of honor."

"I was eight years old, the last time I saw him," said Junior.

"So how did you get to England?" Mr. Windford asked. I have been a slave since I was eight years old, Junior said.

"What! How did you end up that way?"

"I am not sure," said Carlos, but someone sold me as a slave. I escaped some months ago. I was a slave for ten long years."

"Where were you a slave?" asked Mr. Windford.

"In India. It has been a nightmare. I thought it would never end.

"You have saved me from a certain death," said Mr. Windford. "Your father was a great friend of mine. He would help me with my studies. I admired him always. It's absolutely horrible you ended up as a slave. I can't even imagine what you must have gone through.

"I know your father's family came from a lot of money in Argentina. I am happy you escaped, and now you have saved my life. One minute I am riding along the side of the ditch on my horse, and I turned just for a second. The next thing I knew, I was on the ground, hurt and bleeding. I don't know how long I was out. When I came to, I could not move. I was in such a remote area I thought no one would ever find me. At first I would yell for help, but no one could hear me. So I decided to save my energy. Then when I heard you nearby, I gathered up all of my strength and cried out, and you heard me and saved my life."

"It was nothing," said Carlos. "I did what anyone would do given the situation. Anyway, I am glad I could help."

"I am sorry you lost your mother, but I will try my best to help you put all of your sad past behind you," said Mr. Windford. "We will try to get you an education. I will get you private tutors so that you can learn fast, and prepare you for Cambridge

University. We will see if you can shine like your father did. From now on, I will be like your father. You will live in my house. You will be given private lessons. We will get you some new clothing. Do you know how to drive?"

"You mean drive a car?" asked Carlos. "It was the first time I was ever in a car when your chauffeur brought me here," said Carlos. "No, sir, I do not know how to drive. We will get you some especial lessons, so you can learn to drive. We will get you a car. I know my great friend Carlitos would have done the same for me."

Mr. Windford's room door opened just then, and in walked a gorgeous blue-eyed, blonde girl. Carlos couldn't look at her in the face. He didn't know how to act. She looked simply beautiful.

"Hey, Daddy," she said.

"How is my princess?" asked Mr. Windford.

"You are looking much better, Dad. I was missing you so much. We all were looking for you. I am so happy you came home, even if you are hurt. I know you will heal fast. You have always been strong."

"Jenny," said Mr. Windford, "there is someone I want you to meet."

Junior wanted to hide under the bed. He had no idea how to react. He was not used to looking at people in the face. He was used to looking down whenever someone was around. When he was a slave, if he looked up, the owner of the shop would slap him in the face for being arrogant. It is difficult for him to get used to dealing with people in his new life.

"This is Carlos Calderon," said Mr. Windford. "He is the son of my best friend while I was at Cambridge."

She extended her hand and said, "How do you do, Mr. Calderon. I am Jenny."

Junior extended his hand, but it was obvious to all he was very embarrassed and could not look at Jenny in the face. He did not know how to react. He had never seen such a beautiful woman in person.

Mr. Windford noticed how uneasy Carlos was. He decided to call on the chauffeur. "George, why don't you take Carlos to the house, get him some food, and have Rossi give him a room. On the way home, stop by Toni's and get him some new clothing." Mr. Windford then said to Junior, "Go on, Carlos. We will see you again tomorrow."

"Thank you so much," said Carlos.

George and Junior walked out of the hospital toward the car.

"George," asked Junior, "who is the young lady that walked into the room at the hospital? Oh, that is Jenny, the daughter of Mr. Windford. She is his shining star."

"Does Mr. Windferd have other children?"

"Yes, Jenny has a sister named Henrietta. She is a couple years older than Jenny."

"How old is Jenny?"

"I think she is seventeen. Her sister Henrietta is twenty. They are the only two children of Mr. and Mrs. Windford," said George.

"Mr. Windford's wife, Rossi, is a very nice lady. Her daughter Jenny has her character, but I don't know where Henrietta gets hers. Wait until you meet her," said George. "Well, you make up your own mind when you meet her."

* * *

At the hospital room, Jenny asked her father, who was that young man?

Though Junior had looked like he was unsure of himself, he

was really a very nice-looking young man. Three weeks aboard the ship had permitted him to regain his proper weight. He had a nice tan. He was tall and very handsome. His father, Carlitos, had been so handsome, and he had picked an absolutely gorgeous lady, Suzi, to be Junior's mother. Junior had great genes. Aside from being very handsome, he was also very smart, something he inherited from his father.

Jenny could see what a handsome young man Junior was, even though he was not well dressed. *He did not appear like "one of us."* Jenny thought. He looked lost, sad, abused, somewhat confused, and certainly not comfortable with himself. Jenny wondered what was wrong with him, so she asked her father about Carlos.

Mr. Windford said, "He is the son of my best friend from college. He is the son of Carlitos Calderon. His father is from Argentina, and his mother is British. This young man is the person that found me when I had my accident. He brought me home. He saved my life."

"He appears very sad," said Jenny. "He looks like he has some deep emotional pain down in his soul."

"I guess you could say that," said Mr. Windford. "He has been through a lot. He was lost when he was eight years old, sold as a slave, and he endured ten long years of labor. He narrowly escaped slavery after ten years.

"I have invited him to come and live with us at the house. I hope you can help him adjust to his new world. If he is anything like his father, he is a fine and honorable man. Carlos saved my life, and now I have an opportunity to do something for him, so I will do whatever it takes to help him adjust and find his way in life."

Jenny was a kindhearted person. She could not believe what her father had told her. She felt so bad for this poor young man who had spent more than half of his life as a slave. Jenny immediately decided she would try to help Carlos in any way she could.

The next day, she saw Junior at the dinner table. He said hello, and again, he looked down. He could not look at her beautiful face. He did not deserve such beauty, he thought.

"Hello," said Jenny, "how are you?"

"I am fine," said Junior.

At the table, Junior tried to eat slowly, and did not say a word. He knew that he had been eating with his hands for years, and now at this fancy table, with all these different types of silverware, he did not know which one to eat with. Fortunately, he had learned to eat with a fork on the ship. But still, he was lost, and embarrassed. He wanted to hide.

He picked at his food but was too embarrassed to eat. He did not know how to act. He watched as the family around him ate their food, and he tried to learn. He thought that they were all looking at him and how he was reacting. The food looked so good. Junior wanted so much to eat, but he still did not have the courage. He thought he would eventually learn. He would watch and learn.

Jennifer watched this handsome young man with pity—he was so confused and lost. She wanted so much to help him. She just did not know how she could approach him.

After dinner, the family all got up from the table. Junior stayed behind to see if he could help with the dishes. He started to pick up the dishes when Jenny walked back into the room and said, "Carlos, leave that. The help will take care of that."

She added, "Carlos, my father told me all about you and your terrible ordeal. What a sad story. I know it will be tough to get back into a normal life. I will help you. I want to be your little sister, and I am going to help you improve your self-image, and before you know it, you will be one of us, just like my father wants."

Jenny continued, "Today, I give you lesson number 1. You have to look at people in the face. You can't continue to look down all the time. You have nothing to be ashamed of. You can look at people in the face. It's not your fault you were sold as a slave. You are someone special, and you have to realize it."

"It is very hard for me to do that," said Junior. "When I was a slave for ten years, I had to always look down. If I tried to look up, they thought I was defiant, and they would slap me in the face, so I learned to always look down when someone was present, I could not even look at them."

"Well, Carlos, you are not a slave anymore," said Jenny. "You will live the life of a free man for the rest of your life. You have to learn how to live as a free man, and I will help you. We can start right now. Look me in the face."

Junior wanted so much to look her in the face, but he was embarrassed.

"Come on, Carlos," said Jenny, "you can do it." She wanted to see Carlos's face straight on. She had only seen him looking down, and she wanted to look at his eyes and see his face. He was so handsome.

Carlos looked up into Jennie's beautiful blue eyes. He could only look at her for a second; then he looked away. He could not take it. She was so beautiful.

I have no experience with women, and she is so kind to me and so beautiful, he thought. He looked into her eyes once again and wondered what it would be like to hold her hand, to touch her face, and kiss her lips. Junior looked down again.

Jenny said, "It is going to take some time, but we will continue to work on it. You must stop looking down. You must say to yourself, *I am a handsome man, I am not a criminal. I have done nothing wrong, and have no reason to look down.*"

Every night, Junior sat in the parlor, hoping that Jenny would come down and talk to him; and every night, she came down. Soon they developed a great friendship. Junior would dream all day of the moment he would see Jenny. Jenny looked forward to their time together. Often they would go out to the gardens for a walk and look at the flowers and the stars.

Junior began his studies. He had so much to learn—not only about school, but about life in general. He was starting to feel more and more comfortable with himself. Junior studied hard. He was in a hurry to catch up. With private tutoring and his great interest, ability, and determination, he was able to get the equivalence of a high school diploma in two years. At the age of twenty, he was accepted to Cambridge University, where his father had studied more than twenty-five years ago. Mr. Windford had used his influence to get Junior a space in the new freshman class. Mr. Windford had told them that he was the son of Carlitos Calderon, who had been their best student years ago.

Junior was desperate to get ahead. He had lost so much of his life, but finally, he had a chance to make something of himself. He also wanted to show Jenny that he could be someone especial, someone she could be proud of, so he was in a hurry to do something with his life. He studied day and night. The free time he had he spent talking to Jenny. All day he looked forward to his time with Jenny. He thought he could not make it through the day if he did not see her.

Jenny began to see that Junior was someone exceptional. He had great interest in improving himself. He wanted to make a difference in his world. He wanted to make it better than he found it. As Jenny and Junior would talk every night about their dreams, it was a very special time for both of them, and they looked forward to their time together. Junior would tell Jenny that he wanted to become a medical doctor. He wanted to help the sick. He wanted to serve. He wanted to find a way to take away the pain from those that were suffering. He had made up his mind—he would be a medical doctor. Jenny admired that in him.

Junior took his college education very seriously. Just like his father, he excelled in his studies, and it wasn't long before he was the best student in his class. He only had college and Jenny to worry about. She was everything to him. He could not imagine a life without her. He wandered how she felt about him. *Such a beautiful girl who has everything, and I am an escaped slave, he thought. How can I possibly be good enough for her?* Junior began to think that if he worked hard, maybe she would think he was good enough for her.

* * *

Junior finished his freshman class with honors. He had truly enjoyed his first year at the university. Little by little, he was learning to live in his new world. He started feeling more secure. He finally could look at people in the face. His self-image had improved dramatically.

Junior's second year of college was even better than his first. More and more, he was adjusting to his new world. He started to forget his life in India. He did not think of himself as a slave anymore. He stopped having bad dreams that they were coming to get him.

It was all behind him. No more beatings. No more darkness. No more looking down. He was Carlos Calderon, and he was feeling like a new man.

Junior finished college, still number one in his class. He was accepted to medical school. He wanted so much to be a doctor and be able to help those who were suffering.

One night, Jenny and Junior were in the garden, under the moonlight. Jenny looked into Junior's eyes, and she could not resist. She decided she had to make the first move, since Junior had been so traumatized and shy. She thought he would never have the courage to do it.

As the moon shone on Junior's brown eyes, Jenny decided to make her move. She said, "Carlos, you know, your eyes are irresistible in the moonlight."

Carlos said, "Not nearly as beautiful as yours."

Jenny moved close to Carlos and softly touched his face. "You know what I want?" she asked.

Carlos asked, "What?"

"I would love to give you a kiss."

Carlos said, "I would really like that." And then suddenly, and for the first time, Junior kissed Jenny's soft lips, something he had dreamt about for so long. He was, for the first time in his life, holding a woman other than his mother. And she was not only a woman—she was the woman of his dreams.

Carlos held her hand and said, "You know, you are the most beautiful woman I have ever seen, and you are the only woman I have ever kissed. I can't imagine a life without you."

Jenny said, "I have admired you from that day at the hospital, with your dirty clothes, when you could not look at me. Since then, I have been impressed by your desire to improve yourself, and in my heart, I had hoped that you and I will always be together. I have fallen in love with you, and I have dreamt of having a family with you."

Carlos asked her, "Would you marry me, Jenny? Would you be willing to be at my side for the rest of our lives? To walk hand in hand in the good times and in the sad times? To be the mother of my children? To be there when I am ill? Will you grow old with me?"

Jenny said, "That is exactly what I have been dreaming of."

Carlos said, "Do you think your father will let you marry me? Do you think he believes I am good enough for you, after I have been a slave and all the sadness in my life?"

"My father loves you and admires you, and he would be proud to have a son like you."

"Jenny," said Carlos, "let's talk to your father and see if he will consent to our marriage, before I start medical school. What do you think?"

"I think it is a great idea. I want to be with you always." Jenny was running her fingers through Junior's hair. He was holding her hand and looking into her eyes.

Jenny was very proud of Junior. She was amazed at how well he had done in college. No doubt, she really admired him. He had arrived in such devastated state, and now he was the best in his class. Graduated with honors. He would be going to medical school.

Her dream was coming true. She would marry Carlos.

Jenny remembered how she had admired Carlos from the first day she saw him standing beside her father's hospital bed. She was struck by him. He was so handsome, and when she had met him, he could not even look her in the face. *And now he looks at me, and I love looking into his eyes. I want to let him know that I will love him always. I have always wondered does he want a family? Does he want kids? And now I know he wants me and would love to have a family with me.*

Mr. Windford had some gentleman over to his house. They were businessmen, who had come to his home, at Mr. Windford's invitation, for a business transaction. Mr. Windford was buying a mill from these gentlemen. He wanted to process his grains and do the whole process in his own factories. These men had just the equipment that Mr. Windford needed, and Mr. Windford was anxious to move on the sale. He had invited these gentlemen to his home to complete the transaction. They were from out of town and would spend the night at Mr. Windford's house, and in the morning, they would complete the deal and be gone.

It was eleven o'clock at night. Junior had been in the garden with Jenny, and as he was passing down the hall to his room for the night, he heard these gentlemen in the guestroom speaking Spanish. He thought he had forgotten it. He had not spoken Spanish for many years. It was the language of his childhood. He had gone to school in Argentina and had learned to read and write in Spanish. But all of that, he thought, was gone—until this night, when he heard the men speaking Spanish.

He was curious, since he could understand all that was being said. He could not believe he was hearing Spanish spoken after so many years. He was so happy that he could understand what they were saying. He stopped and listened.

He was very surprised, however, by what they were saying.

"Estas seguro que no se van a dar cuenta? Los documentos paracen originales. No hay manera que van a saber que son falsos. Cuando el ya se de cuenta, nosotros estaremos lejos. Es por eso que le hemos pedido efectivo para la transacsion"

Junior heard that the documents they were using were false, and that was why they had asked for cash, and that by the time Mr. Windford realized the documents were false, they would be gone.

Junior was frightened by what he had heard. He needed to speak to Mr. Windford immediately. He did not know what to do. It was late, and he wondered if he would have the courage to knock on Mr. Windford's bedroom door.

Junior knew he had to do it. He gathered all of his courage and knocked on Mr. Windford's bedroom door.

"Who is there at this late hour of the night?" asked Mr. Windford.

"It's Carlos. I need to talk to you about something very important."

"Can't it wait till morning?" asked Mr. Windford.

"No, it can't," said Junior. "It is an emergency."

Mr. Windford opened his door and asked Junior to come in. "What is the problem at this late hour that can't wait until morning?"

Junior said, "You know that I was born in Argentina, where I spoke Spanish as a child."

"Get to the point, it's late," said Mr. Windford.

"Are these men that you are doing business with from a Spanish speaking country?"

"Yes, they are from Spain."

"That is what I thought," said Junior.

"What is the problem, Carlos? Get to the point, it's late."

"Well, I was walking down the hall to my room when suddenly, I heard someone speaking Spanish. I thought I had forgotten it, but when I heard them, I understood every word. I heard them say that the documents they will give you for the mill are false. They said it is the reason they asked for cash. They said that by the time you realize it, they will be long gone. They will be fleeing after the transaction. I am sorry to wake you, but I thought you needed to know before you get involved with these men."

Mr. Windford thanked Junior, and Junior went back to his room.

The next day, before the transaction was to take place, Mr. Windford had alerted the authorities. The police had come to Mr. Windford's house and were ready to intercept the Spaniards, who were about to receive all of this money, only to find the police there. The police were able to identify the documents as false. They took the men into custody. They contacted the real owners of the mill and informed them of what had happened. The mill owners said that they had no intention to sell.

Mr. Windford was very thankful with Junior. He had saved Mr. Windford from losing a lot of money. Suddenly, Junior was a hero. Jenny admired Junior even more.

The next day, Junior and Jenny went over to talk to Mr. and Mrs. Windford. Carlos had asked Mr. Windford if he could have a moment of his time. He said he needed to speak to Mrs. Windford as well.

They met in the parlor. Junior was holding Jennie's hand. He was a little frightened, but he knew what he had to do. Mr. and Mrs. Windford sat across the room. They were surprised to see Carlos holding Jenny's hand.

"Mr. Windford," said Carlos, "I know you have been so kind to me to let me into your home, and you have treated me like a son. It has been several years since I arrived, and Jenny and I, as you know, have been spending much time together, and we have discovered that we love each other, and we want to spend the rest of our lives together. I wonder if you will give me the great honor of having the hand of your precious daughter in marriage. I love her. I will always honor her. I don't have much to offer other than my love and my great desire to have her at my side in life's ups and downs. Will you give me the privilege of having your daughter's hand in marriage?"

Mr. Windford was pleasantly surprised. He turned to his wife and asked, "Mrs. Windford, what do you think of the idea?"

"I think it is a great idea," she said.

"And you, Jenny, what do you think of the idea?" asked Mr. Windford.

"I love him, Dad. I want to be with him always. I want to have his children. I want to wake up in his arms every day of my life," said Jenny.

"I wondered when you two would realize you were made for each other," said Mr. Windford. "Carlos, it will be a great honor, and it would make Mrs. Windford and me very proud and happy to have you be a part of our family. When do you propose to marry?"

"Before I start medical school," said Junior.

"You and Jenny have our blessing, and I am sure Mrs. Windford will be happy to help Jenny, and you do whatever you need to do to plan a dignified wedding that will honor both of you."

And so Junior and Jenny, with the help of Mrs. Windford, planned their wedding. He would invite his classmates, and she would invite her friends and relatives.

Every night, Jenny and Junior would go to the garden and hold hands and share their dreams for the future. They both talked about a big family. He would share with Jenny his dreams of being a doctor and helping those that were suffering and in pain. They could not wait until the day when they could be together, never again to be alone.

Never in the past twenty-four years did Junior have such happiness. He never imagined, when he spent the cold nights as a slave, that someday he would have such fortune. Now it all seemed like a bad dream—a dream he wanted so much to forget.

He finally felt that he belonged. He had been accepted, with open arms, to one of the most prestigious families in London. It seemed that, finally, the world was in the palm of his hands.

Still he wonders how in the world he ended up as a slave in India. Someday, he would investigate.

Though he had no blood relatives, he was now beginning to feel that he had a family. Now at the age of twenty-four, his whole world was coming together.

Junior thought of all the people that had helped him bring this dream into reality. He thought of his friend Henry, who had taken him in and with loving kindness, had taught him to take the first steps. Junior wandered where Henry was. He would love to invite him to the wedding. How destiny had placed the captain of the British ship in his path and somehow had opened his heart to take in a dirty, stinky, feeble person, and given him an opportunity to come to this wonderful country.

Junior remembered how destiny had brought him to Mr. Windford's injured body and given him the opportunity to help him survive. Mr. Windford, who was a friend of his father's, and who had given him an opportunity to start a brand-new life. And now, thanks to him, Junior had found his soul mate. It had been a long road, but the worst was behind him, he thought.

*　*　*

The wedding was a grand experience. The aristocratic families were all there. You could see the long line of limousines waiting to enter the mansion. Men with their black tuxedos and white ties, and women with their long white dresses. The smell of flowers everywhere. Smiles, music, dancing, congratulations, and well-wishes all around.

Mr. Windford had rented the bridal suite at the famous Grand Palace Hotel for the bride and groom's first two nights together. On the morning of the third day, they would board a ship that would take them to Hawaii. They were to board the *Queen Mary* for a trip across the Panama Canal and on to the Hawaiian islands. They had two months before Junior was to start medical school.

The guests had all gone, and finally, there was quiet in the house. Everyone was tired. It was three o'clock in the morning. Jenny went upstairs with her mom to get her things for tonight's wonderful encounter. Mr. Windford took Junior aside to talk to him.

"Carlos," said Mr. Windford, "you now have what I love most

and hold dearest to my heart, my Jenny. Take good care of her, make her happy. Give her all the love and respect she deserves. Never take her for granted. She is used to a lot of attention and admiration and love. I know she loves you dearly and wants to be by your side for the rest of her life. Don't forget, this will always be your home.

"I have personally made all the arrangements for your trip to Hawaii," said Mr. Windford. He gave an envelope to Carlos. "It is a gift to help you with unforeseen expenses. We will be thinking of you every day."

George the chauffeur came down with some suitcases. Jenny came down with her mother, and the two women said their good-byes. Tears fell down Mr. Windford's face as he hugged his little girl.

Jenny and Junior got into the car, and off they went to the Grand Palace Hotel.

* * *

Carlitos finally had his dream of having an airplane factory. He tested every airplane that comes out of his factory. He became well known for his abilities as a test pilot. He had begun making military airplanes that were bought by the US Air Force.

Carlitos had become a US citizen and was very proud to be an American. He had become the best test pilot in the country. He had developed some evasive maneuvers to be used in combat by the military planes.

Aviation was Carlitos's life. He had a degree in aeronautic engineering from Stanford University, so Carlitos understood flying. He was a natural pilot. He thought he had been born to fly.

Carlitos's business was doing well. From time to time, he

would drive down to the Napa Valley to have a bottle of wine and remember his father Ernesto, and how he had such respect and admiration for the wine. After all, his grandfather Fredo's family had been in the wine business.

He would remember the days with Suzi, and how he loved her. He blamed himself for the loss of his son, Junior. He cursed the day they decided to go to India. He tried so hard to put it all behind him, but when he had had a little wine, it would all come back to him with force.

* * *

Jenny was a little tired from the dancing and all the wedding activities. It was an hour's drive to the Grand Palace Hotel. Jenny rested her head on Junior's shoulder. Junior put his arm around her, and they both had a silent moment. Junior wondered what was going on through Jennie's mind. Neither he nor she had ever had a sexual encounter before. Junior wondered how it would go. He remembered the porno movie that he had seen aboard ship of two people having sex. It was the only sexual education he had ever had. He wondered if Mrs. Windford had given Jenny a talk, about what to expect and the role of a woman in a loving sexual relationship. Not having sex, but making love.

Junior thought, *I love her so much. I know it will all work out. I must not worry about it, and let love and nature takes its course.*

Jenny loved to dance, and she was very good at it. She had taught Junior all her favorite steps, and they looked fantastic when they danced together. It had been one of their all-time favorite activities. Long before they committed their love to each other, Jenny had asked Junior to dance with her. At first, Junior did not feel comfortable dancing with her, but soon he discovered that it was a great opportunity to get close to Jenny, so he worked at it, even when he was alone.

Junior had good rhythm and coordination, and dancing came easy for him. He wanted to get it right so Jenny would continue to want to dance with him.

They had practiced a dance to perform during the wedding. It was a fantastic show. The family and the guests were all impressed. They looked so good together.

They both knew they loved each other, and after six long years of being best friends and wanting so bad to be close, their dream had finally come true; and when the priest announced, "Let me be the first to introduce to you for the first time Mr. and Mrs. Carlos Calderon," Junior's heart skipped a beat, and he knew he would love her forever.

Mr. Windford had gotten them the presidential suite on the *Queen Mary*. It was spacious and had a great view of the sea. They had a special garcon that had been assigned to them, to make sure their every wish was met.

*   *   *

Junior's medical school years were very difficult. He dedicated himself to his studies. Jenny would frequently help him, quizzing him and helping him study. Most of all, she gave him the encouragement to go forward.

As usual, Junior was the best in his class. He devoted himself to his studies. He loved medicine. He soaked up like a sponge everything he was taught about medicine. He loved it. Every spare moment he spent at the emergency room or at the hospital, to learn what he needed to be the best doctor he could be.

Europe was in turmoil. Adolf Hitler had begun to invade Europe. England and France, unfortunately, permitted the aggression by the Germans, because they did not want war.

Hitler continued to break all his promises and disregard the peace treaties, and become a force that could not be stopped.

During Junior's second year of medical school, Jenny became pregnant and gave birth to a baby girl, whom they named Suzi, after Junior's mother. Little Suzi had blue eyes and blonde hair. Carlos and Jenny were delighted. Suzi was a happy baby. Often, Junior would sit her on his knee as he studied his books, until little Suzi would fall asleep. Junior was so happy to finally have a family. God had given him this beautiful and kind wife. She had brought him this incredible little person that was part of both of them. His heart was full of gratitude for this fantastic and happy family that God had given him.

On his third year, Carlos started his clinical rotations. He was starting to have firsthand contact with the patients. When he talked with the patients, he always gave them his full attention. He tried to give them hope. He made them feel important. He sympathized with the patients and he let them know he wanted to help. He wanted them to know that he was there for them.

On Junior's final year of medical school, Jenny gave him another gift—a baby boy. They named him David, after his grandfather.

Carlos rotated through his clinical years. He stared with internal medicine, then pediatrics, general surgery, cardiology, pulmonology, psychiatry, dermatology, immunology, ophthalmology, otolaryngology, urology, gynecology, neurology, orthopedics, obstetrics, infectious deceases, hematology, pathology, gastroenterology, vascular surgery, and oncology.

He finally graduated from medical school. He had taken a surgical residency. The war was upon them, and he knew he had to choose the specialty that would be most helpful.

On September 3, 1939, England and France declared war on Germany. They realized that Hitler was not going to honor any of the treaties. He continued invading Europe. England and France had no choice. They had to stop the aggression and the invasion of Europe. They declared war on Germany.

In the USA, the people were divided in their opinion of whether to participate in the war. The news from Europe continued to show German aggression. Soon France would become occupied by the Germans. London began to feel the pounding of the German bombs dropped by the German planes.

Carlitos, who had become a US citizen, decides to help in the British efforts in the war. The airplanes made in his factory were secretly sent to England.

Carlitos decided to volunteer as an instructor and advisor in the British air force. He was initially used only as an instructor for the fighter pilots since he was an expert pilot and had trained himself as a fighter pilot in the United States. Carlitos's role was only in an advisory capacity in the British air force. He was happy to contribute to the war effort. The United States had not yet entered the war, but Carlitos wanted to help.

*   *   *

The Germans continued to drop bombs over London. Carlos decided to send his family to the country. Mr. Windford had a country vacation home, and Jenny, Suzi, and little David, went to the country to join Mr. and Mrs. Windford.

Carlos, now a surgeon, stayed at the hospital to attend to the hundreds of injured who came through the door as a result of the violence of war.

Every day Carlos would operate on dozens of patients injured by the German bombs. He barely had a few hours of rest a day. Still, he wondered about his Jenny and little Suzi and David.

The injured kept coming, and soon again the sirens would sound to announce the pounding of the German bombs. On the streets, people were running everywhere, trying to get to a safe place.

Carlos, who had now joined the British Army, was sent to a field hospital about two hundred miles from London. Every day and night, the injured soldiers kept coming. Carlos never even knew who they were. They just kept coming, and he tried his best to keep them alive.

* * *

On December of 1941, Germany and Italy declared war on the United States, and the United States declared war on Germany and Italy.

The United States suddenly became a war industrial machine, making tanks, planes, armored vehicles, trucks, and all kinds of war equipment needed.

Carlitos had been sending his planes to the war effort long before.

He had been training the British pilots for two years, occasionally participating as a pilot when needed. He had flown several missions and was admired and respected as a pilot and an instructor.

Once the United States entered the war, Carlitos decided to go back home and enlist in the US Air Force. Though he was an older person, because of his experience, they accepted him into the air force. After all, these were war times.

On March 13, 1945, Carlitos was asked to lead a squadron of planes that would deliver their bombs over Berlin. This was a secret mission, and they chose the best pilots and crew. The mission would take place at night. It was a highly dangerous mission, and all the participants had to volunteer to go. They were chosen, but they had to want to go.

Carlitos was proud to lead this group of pilots that had volunteered for such a dangerous mission.

Carlitos must have felt he had nothing to lose. He did not have his family to live for, so he was glad to volunteer for this dangerous mission.

The American pilots began dropping their bombs over Berlin. One by one, they were picked out of the sky by the Nazi guns and planes.

Most of the American planes on the mission had been shut down over Berlin. Carlitos and his crew, as they dropped down to deliver their bombs, had been hit, but they were still flying. Carlitos had taken a large piece of shrapnel that had impacted him in the lower abdomen. The bleeding was intense, and he was losing consciousness. The plane had been badly damaged, and Carlitos and his crew wondered if they would get home. He was unable to pilot the plane anymore. He was very weak and had become unconscious. He had lost a lot of blood and looked very pale.

The copilot was now piloting the plane, he realized the plane was much too damaged to make it to their home base. They asked for permission to land on a nearby British airbase.

The landing strip suddenly lit up. They made their final approach and were able to land the plane.

Suddenly medical personnel were there to take care of the injured. Carlitos was badly hurt, and they took him first to the field hospital. Soon, Dr. Calderon was placing a central line on Carlitos to give him badly needed fluid and blood. Dr. Calderon began to push fluid and blood into Carlitos at a rapid rate. Then they took him to the OR, where Dr. Calderon opened Carlitos's abdomen and removed the piece of metal that had caused the bleeding. Soon Carlitos had a good pulse, and his blood pressure was back to normal.

Carlitos was moved to a recovery room. Dr. Calderon moved on to the next case. Afterward, he tried to get some badly needed rest.

* * *

The pounding by the German bombs continued. Dr. Calderon was working night and day. He tried to get some sleep here and there. The injured keep coming, and he wondered when he would have just a minute to rest.

He was lying on a sofa trying to get some sleep. He was truly exhausted. He could only think about his family—Jenny, Suzi, and David. They were on his mind as he tried to get some sleep. He wondered how they were, and if they had been affected by all the violence he was seeing every day. He wished he could see them, or even talk to them, but there were no phone communications. The Germans had destroyed all communications, and Carlos could only dream about them. He wished he could just touch his Jenny, just for a second. *When will it end?* he thought.

Finally, the Allies made the Germans retreat; and on May 7, 1945, the Germans surrendered, and the Second World War was over.

Carlos was finally reunited with his family. It had been years since he had been with them. Suzi had grown. She didn't recognize her father. David was too little the last time Carlos had seen him, but now he was walking and talking. What a wonderful moment to have his family finally with him. Mr. and Mrs. Windford were also there. They were all so proud of Dr. Calderon. They were in Mr. Windford's home. Part of the Windford estate had been destroyed by the bombing, but the house was intact. The family were all in the garden, enjoying a rare sunny afternoon in London.

* * *

Carlitos had completely recovered and had been discharged. He had decided to buy a vineyard in St. Helena, California. He was done with the airplane business. He wanted to find a place with peace and quiet to spend his days. Still, he couldn't forget his beautiful Suzi, and how she had ended her life. He wandered whatever happened to his beloved son, Junior.

Now that the war was over, Carlitos looked forward to some peace and quiet. He loved going into town. St. Helena was such a quiet and beautiful little community.

He went into the post office to get his mail. He waited until he was home before he opened his mail. There was a letter from the US Air Force. He opened the letter, and saw they were asking him to go to the Veterans' Hospital for a follow-up checkup on his injuries. They told him he may have qualified for some disability.

He glanced at the papers that had arrived and began to look at them in detail. They had sent him his medical history while he was in the air force. There was an accounting of his medical intervention and what his injuries had been. He noticed that his attending surgeon had been Dr. Carlos Calderon. Dr. Calderon had made a short report of his intervention for the medical record. The patients were identified by their tag number and not by their names, and Dr. Calderon had no idea what the names of his patients were. He barely had time to make a small note on each one of them detailing the procedures and what he had found on arrival of the patient and the surgical intervention he had performed.

Carlitos wondered, *Is this a coincidence, or could this be my son. Junior? No way it could be Junior*, he thought. He was lost in India—how could he become a surgeon in England?. Still, thought Carlitos, it is really an incredible coincidence. He decided he wanted to meet this Dr. Calderon who had saved his life.

He wanted to know who this doctor was, and he wanted to meet him, but he didn't know how to find him.

As a retired officer in the US Air Force, he decides to inquire, and asks his commanding officer, who was still in the Air Force, if he could please investigate, and help him find this Dr. Carlos Calderon.

A couple of weeks later, he got a letter that gave him information about Dr. Calderon. They gave him his last known address, the one he had given when he was discharged from the army in England.

To Carlitos's surprise, the doctor's last known address was the house of Mr. David Windford. Carlitos remembered the name from his old college days. He couldn't believe it. It was too much of a coincidence, he thought. He decided to check it out for himself. He booked a passage to London, from San Francisco, on a steamship. On the way to London, he began to dream that maybe this was his son. He did not want to get his hopes up, only to be disappointed. Still, he thought this would be a great opportunity to see his good friend David Windford.

*   *   *

It was a foggy day in London as the ship approached the port. Carlitos had the address written on a piece of paper, and as soon as he got off the boat, he asked a taxi driver if he could take him to the address written on the paper.

Soon Carlitos was standing in front of the mansion he had known so many years ago. It was not like he remembered. Part of the gardens and the guesthouse were being reconstructed, as they had been destroyed by German bombs, but the house appeared the same.

Carlitos went up to the door and rang the bell. The butler

answered and asked Carlitos to come in. He asked if he could see Mr. David Windford. The butler asked, "Who, may I say, is calling?"

"Tell him that Carlitos Calderon is here to see him."

The butler asked again, "What did you say your name was?"

"Carlitos Calderon."

"I shall return in a minute," said the butler.

The butler went into the study and found Mr. Windford. "There is a man at the door looking for you. He said his name is Carlitos Calderon."

Mr. Windford jumped out of his chair and wondered, *Could it be Carlitos?* Mr. Windford went to the door and found his old friend Carlitos at the door. They hugged each other, and tears began to stream down Mr. Windford's face. He said, "Carlitos, I have your son here. He has married my daughter. They have two kids together. Dr. Calderon is at the hospital right now, but you can meet your grandchildren and your daughter-in-law, my Jenny.

"Carlos tried to find you. He found out Suzi had passed, but he never lost hope that someday he would find you. He is the best surgeon in town, and he is loved by his patients for his kindness and understanding. He is due to arrive in a few hours."

Carlitos looked at his delightful grandchildren, and tears came to his eyes.

Mr. Windford said, "This is little Suzi, and this is David."

Carlitos was moved with emotion. He hugged the children and said, "I am your other grandpa."

Suzi said, "I didn't know I had two grandpas."

"You sure do," said Mr. Windford. "And this is my Jenny."

Jenny threw her arms around Carlitos and told him she was thrilled to meet him. Hours passed, and suddenly, they heard, "I am home!" Carlos walked in. "How are my little ones?"

Mr. Windford stepped into the hall and said, "Carlos, we have a great surprise for you.".

Carlitos had followed him into the hall and now found himself looking at his handsome young son, and he was moved with emotion. He cried out as he reached for his son, "My dear son, Junior, I never thought I would ever see you again."

Junior is overcome with emotion himself; he couldn't stop crying. Mr. Windford invites them into the parlor, and then he left to give them some private time alone."

"It's my fault," said Carlitos. "I should have never taken you to India.

"No," said Carlos. "It is all coming back to me. I guess it was too painful to remember, so I had chosen to forget it, but now I remember. You told me to wait at the door of the store. There was a man dancing with a snake, and I stepped out to get a better look. Then another man grabbed me and took me away."

"Your mother and I looked for you everywhere, said Carlitos. We stayed in Bombay for months hoping to find you, but we never did. We had no idea what had happened to you."

"Well, Dad... I have to get used to calling you Dad. I never thought I would ever see you again. But it's all over now. We are finally together."

Carlitos said, "Please tell me. I want to know everything."

"It was terrible. They took me and sold me as a slave. I was a slave for ten years, until I finally escaped. I thought I would spend all of my life there. I had lost hope of ever being free, but the opportunity came one night, and I escaped. I have had very good fortune since. The captain of a British merchant ship offered me a job. I was given British citizenship, since you and Mom had registered my birth with the British embassy in Buenos Aires.

"One day, I found Mr. Windford lying on the ground hurt

after he had fallen off his horse. He had been lying there for two days. I helped him get home, and he took me in. He knew immediately that I was your son. We inquired about you and where you had gone. They said you had sold everything and left without telling anyone where you were going. How did you find me?"

"I was lucky," said Carlitos. "I was lucky because you saved my life."

"Why do you say that?" asked Junior. "Well, during the war, I don't know if you remember, it was all so confusing. People hurt everywhere. One night I was on a mission over Berlin."

"You were a pilot during the war?" asked Junior.

"Yes," said Carlitos. "After your mother died, I decided to become an airplane pilot. I was the oldest officer that was permitted to fly, but because of my experience, they let me participate in this mission over Berlin. Our plane took several hits. Most of the planes went down. I had a piece of metal hit me in the lower abdomen. We made an emergency landing, and I was brought to your field hospital, where you saved my life.

"At the time, I had no idea it was you that had done the surgery on me, but a couple months ago, I received some of my medical files in the mail from the US Air Force. When I looked at the papers, I discovered that the attending surgeon had been Dr. Carlos Calderon. At first, I did not believe it was you, but I asked my commanding officer if he would help me get to know about this Dr. Carlos Calderon. He gave me your address, and I hopped on a boat, and here I am. I never thought I would ever see you again."

Junior said, "I never lost hope. After being a slave for ten long years, and then having such good fortune after my escape, I thought anything is possible. I never gave up hope. I knew I was born to be free."

About The Author

Dr. Barros was born in Bolivia. His parents immigrated to the United States when he was just a boy. They were chasing the American dream. His parents were very poor, with five children to look after. His dream ever since he was a boy was to become a medical doctor. So he began working selling newspapers when he was thirteen years old, and became financially independent from his family at the age of sixteen. He paid for all of his college and medical school education, sometimes by working two jobs. He graduated from the University of California, Irvine School of Medicine. His dream came true when he became an ER doctor at a trauma center which he considers as the most fantastic and fulfilling experience of his life.

Dr. Barros has always liked writing, including medical articles, and he likes expressing himself about life and its beauty, and sometimes its sadness. He is retired now and living in his hometown, where his inspiration comes from the forest, the flowers, the birds, and the butterflies that bring him harmony and beauty and peace and spark his imagination of love and romance-things that people always dream of having in their lives. But together with his appreciation of nature are his memories from so many years of working in the ER, which had brought him face-to-face with the realities of life that sometimes bring sadness, pain, and sorrow.